ELEPHANT WINTER

ELEPHANT WINTER

a novel

KIM ECHLIN

CARROLL & GRAF PUBLISHERS, INC.
NEW YORK

First Carroll & Graf edition 1999

Carroll & Graf Publishers, Inc.
19 West 21st Street
New York, NY 10010-6805

Library of Congress Cataloging-in-Publication Data is
available.
ISBN: 0-7867-0610-4

Manufactured in the United States of America

for Ross who showed me
the marvels of Lake Kariba
&
for my mother who always says
follow your heart

Eli, Eli, lama sabachthani?

That is to say, My God, my God,
why hast thou forsaken me?

—*The Passion of St. Matthew*

CONTENTS

ELEPHANT WINTER

BATTER MY HEART

I am called the Elephant-Keeper, which suits me. My name is Sophie Walker. When I am not at the elephant barns, I live in a crowded house near a tacky commercial tourist farm in southern Ontario. I have a daughter and I take care of the elephants.

I used to read about women who live with animals, women who have followed orangutans and gorillas through sodden rain forests and misty mountains. They talk about looking into the eyes of their animals and seeing the face of God. But I cannot merely observe my elephants, because I feed them, fill their water troughs, shovel their dung, take them for walks and train them to safely carry small children. They dip their knees so that I can climb up their sides to ride on their shoulders. Swaying up there, I hang between heaven and earth. In short, I live with the elephants and they have allowed me into their community.

The elephants have taught me their language. Much of it I cannot hear but I've filled in the spaces with invention,

which is how most people listen to language anyway. The longer I am with them the less invention we need. Wittgenstein said that to imagine a language is to imagine a form of life. But I'm not imagining the elephants. They are really there.

If you choose to live with elephants you've chosen to live enthralled. I allow myself to be ravished by them. I risk their force, to break and blow, to untie and overthrow. I am imprisoned with them and our bonds free us. We have little language for this sort of thing.

The story I am about to tell you is how I came to live with elephants in captivity.

Batter my heart.

SINGING a MAGNIFICAT, CONCEPTION of an ELEPHANT

The place was closed for the season. My mother's house backed on the maple forest at the far end of the Ontario Safari. While she slept each afternoon I watched the elephant-keeper take the elephants on walks through the woods. They rubbed their sides on the trees and scuffed in the fresh snow.

The keeper was a young man who wore his thick grey jacket open to the freezing winds and only a baseball cap pulled down over his long hair. He had high cheekbones and a strong jaw and his blue eyes were wrinkled at the corners from squinting against wind and sun. His jeans were tucked into barn boots but his step was light and his body lithe. He moved with the attractive, loose carriage of men who choose not to submit to offices and desks.

He thought himself unobserved as he rolled up snowballs and tossed them playfully, talking and lightly swaying, at ease in the elephants' company. One of them touched a trunk to his face and he kissed the end and took its tip right inside

his own mouth. That was when he glanced up and spotted me looking at him through the window. I lifted my hand to wave but he turned away and stamped his feet and pulled his meagre hat down over the whitening edges of his ears. He reminded me of young men I had met in Africa, easier out in the bush than anywhere else. He moved away as if to go, and all the elephants moved with him, but then he paused, looked back for me through the glass and beckoned me to come out with his hand. I shook my head, no.

The light over those snowy Ontario fields was short and grey and bleak. We were just past winter solstice and though I'd been home some weeks, I still found it odd to look through the kitchen window and see the curious face of a giraffe above the snowy maple trees. But my mother had always found unusual places to live, and soon enough I was inured even to the swaying grey silhouettes of elephants at play in the snowy fields.

I came home because she was dying. Her breasts were gone, her hair was gone, but nothing they did stopped the cancer. Each morning, after she took her morphine tablet, I arranged her bed table with her sketch pad, some charcoal pencils, and a pitcher of iced tea. She rested most of the day, and when she wasn't dozing she moved stiffly around the house. At forty-nine she had work she still wanted to do. She was impatient with herself and churlish with me.

"Put that carnation in the morphine bottle will you, Sophie, I'm going to draw that after my nap ... aren't they awful flowers? Leave my pad close. Can't you remember

6

to get some grapes? Now get out of here, what do you want hanging around a dying woman. I won't need you until evening. And get this damn budgie off my bed, off you go Henry."

My mother kept twelve budgies and two African Gray parrots. She let all of them fly free in the house. The oldest was Moore, a hand-raised but otherwise ordinary green and yellow budgie. She got him after I left home. She clipped his wings and trained him to land on her bottom lip and peck at her teeth. Slowly his flight feathers grew in again but by then he liked being near her, on her head, her shoulder, her fork. She talked to him all the time but he never learned to speak words back. He clung stubbornly to his squawky budgie locutions, especially when we ran water or closed the back door on its rusting hinges. Now that she was sick, Moore perched on the curtain rod in my mother's bedroom most of the day, and flew at my head whenever I came into the room.

My mother built a large aviary into a wall in the sunroom off the kitchen and added a pretty white and blue budgie called Miranda. The young bird tried to fly at first but she kept bumping into windows and falling stunned to the floor. So Miranda made her world the large cage whose doors were always open and managed to breed with Moore. Her babies learned to fly around the house and each late afternoon when I fed them, Miranda squawked to the others to come back and sat chatting all evening with whoever stayed. My mother regularly visited the bird barns at the

Safari during the off season. She liked trading bird talk with the trainers who specialized in parrots and hawks and kestrels. She charmed them with her stories of Moore and Miranda, and when they had a space problem one winter they asked her if she'd board a couple of African Grays along with her budgies.

The Grays were the colour of clean wood smoke with crimson tails and yellow-rimmed pupils. My mother's pair hung upside down from the living room curtains or spent hours grooming each other on a perch she'd constructed for them in front of the couch. They never responded to their names so my mother called them any paired names she thought of. When she wrote me letters and referred to Abelard and Heloise, or Jesus and Mary, I knew she was talking about the Grays. They were friendly with her and let her scratch between the rows of feathers on the backs of their necks, but they were suspicious and skittish with me. They'd already torn holes in all the curtains and I pushed them off the kitchen counters where they scratched the cupboards foraging for sweet cereals. They stood staring at me defiantly with those intelligent, uncanny eyes and fretted when I sent them scrambling away. One of my endless small chores since coming home was to gather and wash fresh maple and alder twigs for their wooden stand in the living room.

When my mother finally called to tell me about her illness she said, "Soph, they said I'm going to die. I don't know who's going to take care of the birds. Do you think you could come home for a while?"

8

I said I'd be on the next plane and she said, "Oh, I won't die today," and laughed, and I knew she was relieved. But she wasn't ready to die and it was taking longer than we both had thought it would. We hadn't lived under the same roof for years, and after the initial shock, we had to settle into the daily business of waiting. The afternoons when she slept were endlessly long and the wakeful nights longer. I was thirty years old and I still felt as though everything was ahead of me. It was the first time in my life that I'd ever been tied down.

I took aimless walks along Safari Road, staring at the fields and the horse farms buried in snow. Sometimes, during those brief blue twilights, too cold to stay out and too reluctant to go in, I walked around the outside of my mother's house, trying to absorb a bit of warmth from the bricks. I'd stand until I was chilled straight through, unable to give in to or fend off her unwilling dying.

Day after day I watched the elephant-keeper walk his elephants out back behind the maples. I stood in the shadows at the side of the window and I noted how he looked up and searched the reflections in the glass for me. So one day I slipped through the Safari gates, behind a delivery truck stacked with crates of chicks for the big cats. The little birds were mostly frozen and suffocated but a few terrible peeps still escaped the boxes. I ducked behind the trees near the fences, cut through the side field and went straight to the elephant barns. There he was, leading the elephants back from their afternoon walk. His fair hair fell over his forehead and his skin was clear with the rosy dryness of someone who lives outside in the cold. There were white frost patches along the ridges of his cheekbones and he frowned at me. I ignored that, sliding through the fence. I liked him, eyes and bones, so I decided to wait.

The smallest elephant squeezed under the bottom rail like a curious child, and she raised her trunk to scent me. The keeper followed her, reached his hand into her mouth to rub her jaw, and stood between the two of us.

"Can I help you?"

"Not really."

"There's no visitors back here. Who let you in?"

"No one. I didn't ask. That's the house where I live." I pointed with my chin, hands wrapped inside the sleeves of my layered sweaters. "I wanted to see the elephants."

He glanced back through the maples at the dark window sockets in my mother's house. He stared at me, skin flushed, eyes inspiriting me, and said, "I've seen her here before. She used to come to the bird barns. Why didn't you come out?"

"I'm her daughter. She's sick." The words hung cold in the air, untended feelings and questions already between us as if we'd spoken to each other all our lives. "I've just come back from Africa. I used to go see elephants on safari there."

"These elephants are Asian," he said, pulling his hand out of the little one's jaw and rubbing its side. "First time I saw

10

an elephant was the Fort Lauderdale zoo. I stood in front of it all day until my brother came back to get me."

He spoke so softly I had to strain to hear, and his breath froze like crab apples in the air. One of the elephants reached across the fence and ran her trunk tip up the arm of my heavy sweater. The sensitive trunk finger crawled along gently touching and scenting. She got to the bare skin of my neck and she left a sticky shine there, a kind of spit. She startled me but I didn't move. I liked the warm dampness of her touching.

The elephant-keeper was watching me. I waited as her trunk lifted toward my frozen cheeks. She ran it over my face then let it swing back under her. I was caught in her staring eye as if I'd met her before. The keeper's lips loosened upwards with the same affable curiosity I felt in the animals.

"That's her way of finding out who you are," he said.

We stood side by side watching the elephants shuffle against the evening cold and he surveyed them with a chary pride.

"I have to take them in now," he said.

But I wasn't ready to go. I liked the odour of him. I liked the warm animal sweat and hay smells of the elephants out in the frozen air. They waited for him, lightly swinging their trunks through the space around them, over each other's bodies. I soaked up the intelligent calm between them and the peaceable alertness of their keeper. I wanted to touch them myself, I wanted what I felt in them to touch me, and impulsively, I asked him if he needed a barn hand.

He stood gazing into the thin twilight. Animal people see things from odd angles, I knew, because my mother was like that too. Maybe he needed help. I could see him deliberating.

"What's your name?"

"Sophie Walker."

"I'm Jo Mann," and pointing to the elephants, "This little one is Saba, and this is Kezia, behind her is Alice and that one's Gertrude. We've got an African male in the barn called Lear."

I stared at them, trying to take in their names, the shapes of their faces and ears. He said nothing more, and I pulled my scarf up around my mouth and neck against the east wind. He pulled a short stick with a hook on the end of it out from under his jacket and quietly raised it sideways; the elephants began to turn as one toward the barn.

"I'd better go," I said.

He stood for the elephants to pass in front of him, but when I shifted my shoulders toward the front entrance he said, "You don't have to go out by the road. There's a small gate over there in the fence, in the maples just west of your mother's. She knows where it is, she used to use it. You can go straight through," and then, nodding toward the barn, so softly I could choose whether or not I wanted to hear, "Come back . . . I sleep in there at night."

Elephants can move in ether silence, even on crusty snow. I used to hear stories in Africa, fables I thought, about how they'd sneak into a village at night to steal corn and mangoes and not rouse a sleeping soul. These elephants are

Asian. The dry, sure voice butted rudely against my thoughts, which had grown so crisp and clear in the solitude of these last weeks. I could feel Jo's eyes on my back and a few steps further I turned, telling myself I wanted to see the elephants file through the yard into the barn. I searched the barnyard and the stony, snowy fields, but in the half light of winter dusk I could see little and hear only the distant roar of cars. Jo and all his elephants had disappeared traceless in the gloom, gone.

Moore dove at my face and tried to get out the open door. I slipped through like a shadow and the ageing budgie flapped up behind the kitchen curtain in a huff. Other budgies, perched in hollow corners of the house, made a dash for the aviary when they heard me slam the back door. They wanted to be fed. My mother was listening to her beloved Arvo Pärt full blast. She had on the *Veni Sancte Spiritus* from his *Berliner Messe*. The throbbing, insistent strings of the rest of the piece fell away here into a slight melodic line, a lost echo of a folk melody. When the sopranos took over the repeating notes they recalled women who turned in woodlots, and the men chanted back:

Flecte quod est rigidum
fove quod est frigidum
rege quod est devium

(Bend what is rigid
melt what is frozen
rule over what wanders)

My mother didn't make many accommodations for me. She played her music loud, saying it soothed her and she couldn't hear all the low bits, the timpani and basses, if she didn't turn it up. And so I grew to like it too, more for its immanence than for its song.

The Grays were foraging in a pile of cereal they'd spilled on the kitchen floor. A tea bag lay drying in a spoon on the counter and the kettle was still warm. I had asked my mother often not to leave food out but she said the birds got into the cupboards anyway. She was pretending to draw when I went in. Her face was wan. I could read her pain in the papyrus colour of her skin and the depth of the crease between her eyebrows. The room smelled stale but she would never open the windows because of the birds.

"How were your elephants?" she said, barely glancing up.

"Fine, you hungry?"

I wouldn't give her the satisfaction of asking how she knew, of saying I felt spied on. I didn't like this return to us knowing everything about each other.

"No, I'm not hungry."

She lifted her charcoal pencil and sketched, ignoring me. I looked at the table and saw an empty vial discarded carelessly. "Did you take an injection?"

Her extra injections were for what the doctors called

breakthrough pain. She wasn't supposed to use them often. But she said, "What the hell, I'm dying. They're all worried I'll get addicted! Did you ever hear such inanity. They think like well people!"

"How long ago?"

"Don't rag at me, Sophie!"

I turned to go make us some supper, and staring at her charcoal she said, "Get me fresh ice."

I snapped back, "I'm not your slave."

"A glass of water! I'm thirsty."

Our house was always full of people coming and going, neighbours, students debating odd ideas, young women who fluttered around her, the kitchen busy with food other people prepared, big books of pictures spread out, excitement pulled through the rooms. When I first got back I didn't understand its stillness. I thought bitterly that people were afraid of death but it was more that she wouldn't tell people. She didn't answer the phone and when they came by she'd say she was busy or fend them off with silence. She behaved the way she did when she was working on a new canvas, waiting without distraction. I hadn't realized in these past years she'd become more and more solitary. She had a tart tongue and a critical agility of mind that I'd found difficult as a teenager. But after I left home and began visiting again, we talked about art and travel and men and our lives as two women connected by blood and love, we drank scotch together, her advice no longer law, her urging no longer urgent. It was then our friendship began. And this last time I came back, it was only me she wanted to let touch her secret. She didn't trust easily and she didn't trust many, this was what I was learning about the mother I'd always thought so sociable. Living together again after all those years we often chafed at each other's presence, though she wanted me near and I wanted to be near. I told myself I only needed a bit of air and something else to do.

She frowned at me and said, "Trailing after circus elephants! Have you ever seen one of their shows? Tacky rubbish."

Once she would have lightly turned and left the room after a remark like that. The cruelty was that now I left. After coming so far to be with her, I turned and stalked mutely out and she lay trapped in bed by her own pain.

———◆◆◆———

In Zimbabwe I taught art and was working on a series of sketches of the cave paintings of Matopos. I'd gaze at the line drawings of prehistoric men hunting, watched over by strange stars and mythic creatures, and pull ticks out of my clothes. I sketched quickly before the sun got too hot, listening to the hum of insects and wind in the dry grasses. I lived alone in Bulawayo for three years in a small rented cottage. I kept dogs to ward off the puff adders and mambas who liked to sun themselves on my window sills. About once a year a snake got one of the dogs. There were big fields out back, planted with corn and forbidden crops of dagga. I lived in a motley community of expatriates and Africans and we all kept each other company, fell in and out of love, ate together, drove on camping safaris whenever we could. I liked my messy kitchen and makeshift rooms cluttered with paints and sketch pads. I liked how people didn't knock but drifted around doorways and slid against a wall waiting to be offered a glass of beer or water. We organized our lives around getting out to the bush to watch the animals and birds, me to sketch my cave paintings. On the big trips we'd drive out to see lions and kudu or take punts on rivers and lakes to look for hippos and water buffalo. From Bulawayo we could escape in the evenings to sit on old trucks and watch a tree full of male weaver birds making endless nests trying to please a female. I often sat up all night and left just before dawn to scramble along the edges of the caves to sketch and photograph the cave paintings. When I wasn't teaching I slept during the hot middle of the day, roused myself at dusk like the animals to drink water and work again. I liked the exotic heat and sitting on our porches at night, watching for snakes in the garden, sleeping little and making love more or less with whoever stayed.

Back here, my mother's house was isolated at the end of the long rural road. The snowplows had to take care not to block our driveway with banks of snow. The earth was not rich enough for good farming but a few places struggled along with pumpkins and cucumbers; it was a better horse area. White fencing stretched like tape measures over the snowy terrain. Straight-backed youngsters glued to their ponies moved around striped barrels and over cedar-rail jumps while their parents watched from kitchen windows. On my mother's patch of land was a tumbledown vegetable garden and a small outbuilding she'd turned into a place to paint. It was the first time in her life she'd been able to afford a separate studio. When I was growing up, she painted on porches and in back bedrooms and she supported us with her teaching. But in recent years there had been a small vogue in the highly realistic wildlife painting she did. She made enough money to drop her daily teaching, but her work didn't sell briskly because her migrating birds perched on clotheslines hung with socks, her foxes sniffed around compost heaps, and her favourite red-tailed hawks swayed on television aerials and light posts. The critics praised her technique but her gallery encouraged her to leave out the domestic details—the laundry and fences and wire. I never understood that. Her pictures were the world I grew up in which didn't seem spoiled at all. I liked what she did and learned how to do it so I could do it too.

Since I'd come back into the deep snow and darkness I hadn't worked much. I tacked up my cave paintings on my bedroom walls, but the reddish, angular figures and the mythic animals retreated away from me into their distant world. Even the charcoal that looked so black in the hot sunlight of Bulawayo seemed indistinct and faded here in a house where someone was dying. As I poached eggs for us and made some toast, I resolved to stay awake all night as I had stayed awake through the darkness so effortlessly in

18

Africa. Perhaps all the sleep was making me witless; I didn't need so much slumber.

Just before midnight, shivering under the frozen chips of stars, I hurried away from the house over the dry snow, found the gate in the back fence and struggled with the icy hook. I hurried over the beaten elephant path toward the barn, lifted the heavy latch and slipped through the door. The inside was warm and fragrant with elephant flesh after the odourless cold outside. I stood smelling and waiting for my pupils to open, searching the darkness, looking for where he slept. As I stood I felt an odd pressure change against my eardrums. I heard an elephant shift on her feet and I could make out the shadowy bulk of the others, standing and lying, their ears silently spreading, their trunks lifting and turning toward me, scenting. Again I felt that subtle push against my eardrums and then it was gone. I know now the elephants were rumbling to each other in sounds I could feel but not hear.

Finally I began to edge toward Jo's cot on the west wall. My winter boots brushed against the hay and the floorboards squeaked. I heard one of the elephants moving toward me and I squeezed myself against the wooden planks. There was a skittish feeling in the barn that I didn't like. I could see the shadowy shapes of their trunks lifting and scenting, trunks so powerful they could knock me out.

The elephants were agitated now, rolling up to their feet, snorting and flapping their ears.

I pressed on to the back corner where Jo was awake and up on one elbow, the blankets pulled back for me. I dropped my thick coat to the floor, slipped out of my clothes and got into bed with him. Our faces were close enough to kiss but instead he traced his finger over my lips and cheeks and forehead then back down my arm. He blew on my lips, and dry with winter and parched, they filled with blood. His skin smelled of the barn and his long hair fell back on the rough pillow. At the first touch of his lips on my wrist I exhaled again.

He whispered, "I didn't think you'd come."

I felt his lips, propitious and warm on the side of my neck, in the hollow of my back, across my thighs. The sound of the elephants' ears lifting and falling against their necks, their rumbles and whistles and sighs went through me like a song beyond the genius of breath. I lay under Jo, his body warm and light as down, teasing and tempting, and then he rolled me on top of him and my skin hot I pushed the rough blanket off to the side. Kneeling above him, my head bent over his neck, I felt a thick wet touch on the naked skin of my back between my shoulders. I froze still as a snowbank. A damp trunk finger was tracing along each vertebra of my spine, all the way to my own curled-under tailbone.

Without moving I whispered into Jo's ear, "One of them's loose."

I heard the lightest of laughs, really only a breath, and Jo said, "It's Kezia. She doesn't like to be left out."

"I thought they'd be shackled at night."

He brought me down on his chest, and he reached for the scratchy blanket to cover me. Gently he brushed Kezia's trunk aside. "She's always been able to unshackle herself…" He raised up on one forearm and said quietly, firmly, "Back Kezia!"

The elephant moved off, a noiseless shadow passing to the far side of the barn. I lay in the darkness that night with Jo for as long as I could. When I closed my eyes I felt Jo's touch between my fingers, along the edge of my scalp, filling me, but I kept seeing Kezia's clear gaze through the darkness. I listened to the creaking of the barnboard, to the breath of the elephants, to the cracking of frozen branches outside. I could feel the elephants rumbling as if chanting to both of us. For as long as I could I lay listening to all the sounds of the barn and beyond.

We can hear howling winds and we can hear grass brushed by snakes and crickets rubbing their feet and frog songs outside at night. We can hear the wings of a dragonfly and the breath of a new lover and the sigh of the dying, but there is sound all around us that we cannot even hear.

<hr />

After that first time I went to the barn every afternoon, and whenever I could at night. The females slept and rested in a single open area in the centre of the barn and Lear, the Safari's only male, stayed in one of the two stalls on the side. Jo showed me how to muck out the barn and the barnyard then left me with my pitchfork and shovel while he took the elephants out for their afternoon walk. The water troughs were connected to pipes running underground. Long-handled brushes for the elephants' daily scrub hung on one wall, and the pitchforks and shovels were kept in a locked cupboard. He showed me his bag of tools for their feet: the draw knife to smoothe their leather-ish pads, a large rasp for trimming their toenails. The harnesses and howdahs hung in a tack room opposite Jo's cot. Upstairs he stored hay and grain, which was dropped down through a chute. Wide cracks between the rich grey barn-boards softened the shafts of outside light, and high above in the frozen rafters, two winter owls wove a whole and separate life.

Jo was sleeping in the barn because Kezia was expecting.

"After the baby's born," he said, "I'll be here about six months, unless it's early and we're in circus season. Some-one they know should be here to keep the barn calm. When Saba was born, she was so small she couldn't reach Alice's tits. I had to pump Alice's milk and bottle-feed her for a month until she got tall enough."

Jo had been trying to breed his elephants since he'd come to the Safari. Even this most ordinary mystery was delicate and dangerous in captivity. Agitated elephants had to be moved in trailers away from home and then, if they bred, the mother waited twenty-two months while her baby grew. There were heartbreaks, dangerous males, miscarriages, bad births.

I learned to move slowly among the elephants. Saba was the youngest at eighteen months. She was spoiled by all of them but especially by Alice, her mother, and Kezia. At thirty Kezia was the eldest, and had taken the position of matriarch. She was the only elephant who'd been born in the wild. Her mother had been caught for work in the Indian bush and Kezia was later taken from her and shipped to England. Since then she'd been bought and sold by two zoos and a safari. She hadn't had a baby yet, though she'd miscarried several times.

Gertrude had a big tear in her left ear. She was born in a lumber camp in Thailand and was one of the last Asian elephants to be brought to North America. Inventive and witty, she was the first to learn how to unpin the barn door hinges. She had a particular passion for old tires. Jo kept a few in the corner of the barn for them to play with. Gertrude lifted them with her trunk, tucked them under her belly and rolled on them. She also liked to squeeze them through the stall bars and wear them on her head as a hat.

Lear, Jo's favourite, was the only African elephant.

"He's mine, this one," said Jo. "Most places don't want a male. African males aren't much good when they hit their twenties. They get unpredictable. I took him when no one else wanted him."

With Lear, Jo showed me the simple voice commands

they all knew: steady, move up, lie down, trunk up. Jo was disciplined with them and he never asked more than he needed, even to show me. He'd taken on their gentle, intelligent ways.

"If you listen they'll tell you what you need to know," he said. "If you think you understand something they're not saying, it will make them uneasy, or afraid."

"How will I know?"

"How do you know if you make me uneasy?"

I thought, "Do I?" and said, "I don't know. I suppose I watch for little signs . . ."

"It's about the same with elephants."

"But I don't know how to read them."

"You will."

As I watched Jo and the elephants I began to see the language between them. The only tool Jo used was an ankus, a short stick with a hook on the end of it. He touched Lear's leg with his ankus in the field and Lear understood the touch as the first word in a long idea that began with him dipping his knee so that Jo could scramble up his side for a ride back into the barn. But Lear understood a similar touch in the performance ring to mean he should kneel for a bow. It was an elephant homonym; the signal sounded the same but meant different things in different contexts. The complex language between Jo and his elephants had as much moral responsibility as any human communication. As long as they both agreed on the conventions and certain fixed ideas of their mutual responsibility they could live together peaceably and creatively. But if either broke the code, asked for something unreasonable, failed to answer out of plain churlishness, there was failure. Through language they explored each other. If one of them refused to listen, pretended he couldn't speak, the other was betrayed.

Jo taught me their routines. Each morning he bathed them, made sure their feet and toenails were in good shape, then fed them and worked them for the demonstrations. He showed me the screw in the clevis, the U-shaped iron leg shackle that some of them learned to undo. He used the solid brummel hook on Lear, impossible for an elephant to open. He showed me how he mucked out and where he walked when he took them to the fields each afternoon. I observed his constant alertness among them, reading their moods and their intentions. His days were long and physical and busy.

"In a couple of months I'll hire them out for six weeks of circus," he said, "and when the Safari opens again we take them to the pond twice a day for a swim, put on the two shows every afternoon and give rides." He reached for me. "But winters are slow."

The barn was fresh and cool after my mother's stale bedroom. We leaned against bedding straw, Jo slipping his arm behind my back and drawing me close. His ways were so soft that the hard strength of his arms kept surprising me. In his slow, quiet voice he teased, "How did you know I was looking for a barn hand?"

I laughed and shot back, "So this is how you train your help!"

His jaw tightened against my alacrity and I felt his awkwardness when words flew too lightly back and forth. But he shrugged it off and said peaceably, "I never thought you'd come back that night."

"But you asked!" and then I too refrained from speaking.

Since I'd taken over the mucking out, he spent longer walking with the elephants in the fields. On the coldest days he left Saba and Alice with me. I brought some books and pads of paper and a big old tape recorder from the back of one of my mother's closets to listen to music while I cleaned the stalls. Each afternoon I hurried through the shovelling and cleaning and settled down on a bale of hay to sketch. I drew the elephants, a pair of old barn boots, sacks of grain, the owls, our threadbare blankets. I wasn't much taken with the inside of the barn but I began to notice how the slats in the walls made for play in the light, how the stalls and bins and doors divided the space. I worked thoughtlessly, jotting down notes about the elephant sounds, about what I was reading, words, pictures all jumbled together. I threw the pages into a big box as fast as I made them and I began to understand something of my mother's impulse to put our laundry baskets and cracked pots into her paintings.

One late afternoon I'd finished the barn work and I was listening to Pärt's "Silouans Song" and sketching. The recording I had was one of my mother's, made at Lohjan

Kirkko in Finland. Between phrases, Pärt let the reverbera-
tions of each note echo against the old stones of the church
where they'd recorded, and when the sound was gone I
could hear the brush of hair against the strings. Pure round
voices rose in shafts of simple triads, and between the
phrases of this song without words I could hear snow falling
outside and the sound of my charcoal on paper. When I
closed my eyes I could see mandalas and carved saints and
rough stone arches. Nothing could be asked and yet everything received. It was music to make oneself ready.

I sat on a bale of hay sketching a piece of rope and Saba
was bothering me. I brushed her trunk away gently but she
nudged in again and picked up one of my charcoals and
tried to drag it across the barn floor. It broke, but it left a
trace there and she ran her damp trunk over the trace and
smudged it. I watched as she picked up the broken charcoal
and tried to make another mark. I'd read that elephants
draw but Jo didn't have much time for that sort of thing.
He said, "I like them the way they are, not because they do
what humans do."

I sat and watched Saba scratching on the floor. I uncapped a marker that wouldn't break so easily and handed
it to her. I tore a piece of paper off my pad and laid it on
the floor. Her touch was too hard and though she made a
mark she ripped the paper. Then she put the marker in her
mouth to taste it.

I held another piece of paper against my chest. Now Saba
had two purposes: to make a mark on the paper and not to

hurt me. She thought about her problem for a while, lifted her marker and, as if she were lightly running the tip of her trunk over me, she made a line. I held my breath and kept the paper still. She dropped the marker and ran her trunk over her line, picked up the marker again and deliberately made another line, this time more confidently. Then she scribbled lightly across her two lines, like a child, tickling me and I laughed.

Once she understood the right amount of pressure, one after another she drew on the six different sheets I had laid on the floor. Then, tired of it, she dropped her marker and walked back to Alice, scooped up a trunkful of hay and began to eat. I scooped up Saba's drawings and put them in my bag.

<hr/>

"Do you want to go for a drive this morning?"

"It's cold."

"I know. We can wrap up. I'll get the car started."

My mother stood in front of the door, eager to go out, while I layered us in scarves.

"Sophie, I can't breathe with all this wool over my mouth."

"You won't be able to breathe in that cold air, either!"

"You sound more and more like a mother."

"God forbid!"

We got in the car and drove down Highway 6 through

the layers of blasted-out limestone. The exhaust from the cars froze and trailed behind each tailpipe like cotton batting and puffs of frozen white smoke perched on the top of every chimney. We stopped on the big docks at LaSalle Park where dry-docked boats were stacked behind fences and covered with great sheets of canvas along one side of the pier, and we sat looking through the windshield at the steel mills across the frozen bay. Most of the boys I grew up with had worked in the mills through summers and holidays. They learned to drink beer with the men and to rein in their strength so the old men wouldn't have to work too hard when they left. They learned to sleep in hidden nooks in the factory and keep an eye half open for the floor managers on night shift. After they'd been in the mills they were better lovers and they behaved badly in school. My mother's father worked there his whole life. I knew she liked to look across and feel that odd jarring sense of having left behind what once had been your world. And now dying she looked back there to remember her father. When I was younger and we had picnics and sketching afternoons on this shore, I once said, "Too bad the steel mills make the shore so dirty and ugly," and drawing them furiously she snapped, "It's honest dirt over there!"

We watched winter ducks skid across the ice, searching for bread, their breath freezing in two little white pearls on the tops of their beaks.

"Yesterday Gertrude turned on the inside water tap and flooded the barnyard."

29

"Maybe she wants to skate," she said.

"When Jo took them out, they broke up the edges and started sucking on the ice cubes, so he threw some fruit in buckets with water and made them popsicles. They loved it."

"Clever elephant man . . ." she sniffed.

We were used to being active people. We didn't know what to do with so much time on our hands.

I told her about learning to train Saba.

"She'll walk with me now. We're going to start putting sandbags over her shoulders to teach her to bear a little weight. They teach them the trunk up command with jelly beans. I have to stand on a ladder to get her to raise her trunk high enough. I'm amazed at how she takes to it."

"A little genius," said my mother, and then more curious, more like herself, "I suppose they're used to thinking about how to find food or where water is or how to get their babies out of trouble. There's not enough to think about in a tourist safari." I'd turned the motor off and the car was growing chilly. She pulled a scarf over her mouth and spoke through the wool, "The smaller the cage the more we need something to meditate on." She shifted on the car seat away from me, turning her profile to the steel mills across the lake, and said, "Be sure to give your little genius lots to think about."

Jo was not the sort of man I was used to. He barely spoke. He didn't read. He didn't care about the rest of the world. He grew up in a trailer camp and at fifteen got himself into a circus to learn about animal training. He bought three bear cubs, a trailer and a big cage and taught himself how to train them for a bear act. But what he really loved were the elephants, and each evening after he'd put the bears to bed, he worked at the elephant tent. By the time he took them over he had trailered circus animals from Alaska to Texas. And after a decade of sleeping in the backs of trailers, Jo had a modest dream: he wanted to live in one place with elephants. But zoo people look down on circus folk who live and sleep and eat with their animals.

Jo never got the kind of schooling a zoo keeper has, but when he heard about a trainer killed by an elephant in a small Florida zoo he got on a plane and presented himself the next day. They'd shot the animal, a nineteen-year-old African male, and there were two others that everyone was afraid to go near. Jo took over, worked them, taught them to give rides and made his reputation in the tiny world of elephants. He was finally hired by the Ontario Safari to come north from Florida and here he created a family of elephants who rumbled with loud affection each time he came into the barn. The Safari let him do what he wanted, provided he could raise enough money in circuses to support the elephants.

He didn't really care what I thought about anything unless it was about the elephants. He was uncomfortable indoors and his opinions were strong. When promoters and community organizers who wanted to hire his elephants came around he hardly spoke at all, except to pronounce strict rules about what they would or would not do. He showed no interest in the books I'd stacked near his bed and he appeared not to listen when I told him that I was reading about elephant infrasound, rumbles too low for humans to hear. Still, when I brought in a powerful microphone and recorded the silence among the elephants, he didn't stop me. I played it back to him sped up and we listened together intently, hearing for the first time the distinct low rumble that is Elephant. We identified the roar of the electric light and the thudding flap of elephant ears. Their breathing sounded like long slow wheezes, but wound into all that din of background noise was Elephant, like a rhythmic double bass, theirs alone to hear.

"Do you think they know we don't hear it?" I asked Jo after the first time we listened.

"Hear what?" he said.

"Their language."

"Could be their bellies rumbling for all you know."

He knew it wasn't, I could tell by the intent way he listened, but he was a resistant thinker, careful and slow and not given to leaps or dreaming. He knew what he discovered through his own experience and that he knew exquisitely.

"I want to record more, Jo, see what I can find out."

"Suit yourself," was all he said, undoing the buttons on my sweater.

Of course I nearly always did. Each day after mucking out I recorded the elephants and I kept reading. I started fiddling with putting the sounds they made into some kind of order, translating them, arranging them like a dictionary. Elephant is a peculiarly difficult language because they communicate most richly in "paunsing," low-frequency sounds we can't hear. Sometimes I can feel pressure changes in the air when they are rumbling and I can see vibrations under the skin on their foreheads. They paunsed whenever Jo came into or left the barn. They paunsed to each other when they woke in the morning, as they walked, when one of them was outside and the others in. I could feel them when we were in Jo's cot together. They appeared to be standing silently when they were, in fact, talking together.

Before Jo got back, I always put the recorder away with my sketching and the pitchfork and shovels. Each early twilight, when I got up from his cot and made ready to return to my mother's, I could already feel the prints of Jo's hands on my body wearing off and my yearning beginning all over again. I wanted more of him, and on the next cloudless winter day, I came in from the sun-planished snow and said to him, "I'm not staying inside today, I'm coming with you."

Jo walked into the back of the tack room and came out with two pairs of snowshoes. "We'll go to the north fields then," he said, "they'll like the change."

He helped me adjust the straps and laughing I walked bowlegged out into the fields. I learned to sway a little, taking

33

longer, lighter strides. We snowshoed beside the elephants away from their usual path, away from my mother's back windows, and excited by the change in routine they tossed snow over their necks and lifted their faces to the sun. We followed the back fences and slid down into a gulley where no one could see us. Jo's face was bright and boyish in the cold. He lifted his hands unconsciously to me. Under the elephants' tutelage, we too had become a species of touchers, tangled up together. I could feel him through our layers of winter clothes, thick coats and mitts squashed between us, lips warm, cheeks nipped and white. The cold held us out naked and we wrapped ourselves up in our own warm breath. Lying side by side in the snowbanks watching the sky, listening to dead leaves crick at the ends of their branches, I wrapped Jo's hair round and round my fingers, his body round and round mine until, too soon, the sun fell and the temperatures dropped and the elephants got hungry. We got up and in the shock of not touching we began to run back.

I watched Jo leading the elephants, nimble and disappearing. The muscles of my legs ached and I fell behind. Kezia slowed and touched her trunk to my arm to encourage me through my weariness. We followed the others and alone out there in the waning light I looked beyond to the jut of the great escarpment with its old gnarled fir trees. Then Kezia touched me again and I shifted my attention back to the confines of the electrified fences, to the corrugated steel barns where the animals endured our long winter. I couldn't help but think, "It's such a tawdry place."

34

It might have been that afternoon that I got pregnant.

I didn't know what to tell Jo, what he might think. I had no intention of staying with him and sleeping in a barn for the rest of my life. But the more I thought about this baby the more I wanted it. I knew that babies and men and work don't go together very well, but you have them all anyway. You can't wait forever. I thought I'd just take my baby wherever I went. I'd made a habit of moving around, of leaving men, and I figured as soon as my mother was dead I'd leave again.

ELEPHANT-ENGLISH
DICTIONARY

Prepared by Sophie Walker

Preface

It is the fate of those who toil at certain employments to be driven by inner yearnings more than buoyed by the world's approbation, and to be exposed to censure with little hope of praise. Among these I count myself, a humble elephant-keeper and amateur lexicographer of the Elephant language.

A dictionary of the Elephant language is to some extent different from that of other dictionaries in so far as the uses and pleasures of Elephant differ from those of French, English, Ojibway or even Latin and Greek. The study of Elephant has the added difficulty that our human limitations (no trunk) prevent us from communicating fluently in Elephant. And so I stand before this task in the melancholy knowledge that whatever I may do to illuminate the Elephant language, an elephant will never speak my language and I will never speak hers.

The vocabulary of this dictionary is drawn uniquely from

the elephants at the Ontario Safari who come from Thailand, India and Florida, and have no doubt been influenced by their contact with Africans. What has transpired at the Safari, I believe, is a unique creole, a result of transplanting, blending and mixing.

Elephant is a highly adaptable language.

Transcription and the Elephant Spectrogram

Human speech is created by combining the physiological possibilities of the nasal cavity, hard palate, teeth, lips, tongue (blade, front and back), soft palate, teeth-ridge, uvula and vocal cords. Elephant infrasound is created by vibrations at the top of the trunk, which can be seen in the thin layer of skin fluttering in the forehead. High frequency (322-570 Hz.) screams, bellows, trumpets and calls can be heard by the human ear, but the low dominant frequency (18-35 Hz.) of their rumbles was first picked up as the upper harmonics of intense infrasonic communication and cannot be heard without the enhancement of sped-up recordings. The most accurate means to transcribe Elephant is by use of a spectrogram. For the general reader I have adapted the more familiar roman alphabet since the International Phonetic Alphabet (IPA), even with its wide analysis of sound, resists certain Elephant sounds—rumbles, screams, whistles and trumpeting. Immediately after each vocalization I record the hertz range, which indicates if it is audible to the human ear.

Speech Acts

Western language is about "naming things" (nouns), "doing things" (verbs) and all the ways in which those two activities are amplified (conjunctions, adjectives, adverbs, pronouns, objects, etc.) In contrast, Elephant is about "being" and "being together (surviving) in community." Since language and behaviour are inextricably linked, this single idea is fundamental to understanding not only Elephant language but also Elephant culture.

Few human languages place as great an emphasis on communal well-being as Elephant, but there are traces. For example, in the African language, Shona, it is awkward and impolite to enter into any social interchange without first asking after the health of the interlocutor's spouse, children, mother, father, aunts, uncles and other extended family. Ritualized verbal concern for the other is also clear in the Shona morning greeting, "Hello, did you sleep well?" and the standard response, "Hello, I slept well if you slept well."

A typical Elephant speech act is characterized by a high level of repetition and formality. Greetings and empathetic enquiries and responses are repeated often throughout the day. Much Elephant discourse is aimed at members of the group keeping in harmonious contact with each other and is woven into chants, songs and communal rumbling.

All this said, the communal nature of Elephant does not preclude the use of the language in a solitary way for the purer pleasures of language. I wish to emphasize that a verbal elephant is perfectly capable of a soliloquy, an apostrophe, a meditation, a prayer or, if you will, talking to herself.

More Sense Less Syntax

Cicero, in 46 B.C., advised us never to translate *verbum pro verbo* (word for word), and almost twenty-one centuries later the advice still holds. In each definition I have tried to identify a corresponding range of human feeling, sensation or thought. Wherever translation questions have arisen I have opted for sense over strict adherence to a particular word or etymology.

Language is a continually shifting thing. Let it not be forgotten when omissions and errors are found that the Elephant-English Dictionary has been written with little assistance or patronage, far removed from academic shelter, amidst the inconvenience and exigencies of a commercial safari in an obscure corner of Ontario, in sickness, sorrow and the distracting joys of pregnancy, birth and child-rearing.

I offer it up then to the interested reader with little to fear or hope.

Words slip and slide.

PART ONE

Formal Greetings

In Elephant, Formal Greetings are vocalized at many times during the day—upon waking in the morning, before eating and after any separation, even those of short duration. They are uttered frequently, known and used by all members of the group and articulate a strong group coherence.

I have seen our matriarch, Kezia, train elephants new to the group in these greetings. In one case, an elephant who had been isolated for many years was billeted with us for three months. For the first few weeks she was afraid of the others, stayed away from them, and though she didn't talk she listened intensely. Kezia cornered her in the yard one day, greeted her with the formal greeting rumble, then forced her trunk into the stranger's mouth (which is part of the greeting speech act). She kept repeating this until the newcomer extended her trunk into Kezia's mouth. After she had learned this most basic of Elephant civilities, she was able to browse in the yard and sleep in the barn with the others.

Signs and Other Conventions

^ sharp intake of breath to break a rumble

~ slow, steady building of sound into lengthened paunsing

* indicates a word or form combined with another to create a new locution

~ah: (14 Hz.) Dawn greeting to the sun, usually with the trunk stretched up and out toward the east.

The Romans believed that the elephant worshipped the sun, moon and stars. They minted a coin showing an elephant with its head lifted to the heavens. Aristotle, Alexander the Great's tutor, described the elephant as "the beast that passeth all others in wit and mind ... and by its intelligence, it makes as near an approach to man as matter can approach spirit."

~am: (7 Hz.) An evening salute.

This sound is made precisely at dusk if the day has been a contented one, expressing harmony with nature *(see ~ah)*. The feeling of this utterance is captured in the story of Pu K'ung, a Tantric monk who joined in meditation with elephants in order to shift the clouds. Most elephant-keepers, including me, hold in disdain people who romanticize elephants, but I have seen my elephants singing this evening song into the grey Ontario winter twilight. Their bodies appear to soften and shift like clouds on the rocky fields.

mrii: (20-30 Hz.) Greeting rumble.

In all the hours of Elephant I have heard, I love this rumble best. Elephants are big animals who like to do things in a big way. Though they may have been apart only a half hour they greet each other loudly using a combination of the *mrii* rumble with various expletives *(see *grht, *whit, *rii)*. They rumble and put their trunks in each other's mouths, shake their ears, urinate and defecate and stamp their feet. Watching them together makes me feel whole. When I see them greeting each other so exuberantly, celebrating each other's lives daily, I know love is possible.

mrii~ahah: (18 Hz.) Morning greeting rumble.

Adult elephants sleep only a few hours at a time. But through the night there is a slowing of activity and they take turns dozing and sleeping more deeply. In the morning, they greet me and each other with this morning rumble and touch each other (and me) with their trunks. It is a moment of great sensual and emotional pleasure and sets a wonderful tone for the day.

grht: (20-35 Hz.) A greeting for a special friend or family member.

All members of the group tend to like each other, and they nurture their bonds of affection with constant and caring attentiveness, but they do not love each other indiscriminately.

hrhrhrhr: (20 Hz.) An expression of longing.

When our elephants used to be taken away for several weeks to the circus, those left behind would stand where the trailers were and rumble this. If an elephant-keeper is separated from the elephants, they often rumble *hrhrhrhr* throughout the day. The call is deeply rhythmic, as if pulled by forces beyond life. It reminds me of Pound's translation of "The River Merchant's Wife: A Letter."

> If you are coming down through the narrows of the
>   river Kiang,
> Please let me know beforehand,
> And I will come out to meet you
> > As far as Cho-fu-Sa.

Ooo ahahah~whoo aaoh: (15 Hz.) Deep rumble which probably means, "I'm here, I'm for you (as nature would have it)."

This greeting is used when elephants have come to help one another. Gertrude rumbled this to Lear when he was sick. I have also heard it rumbled to babies who are afraid or uncomfortable. When I hear it I think of Emily Dickinson's rhythms and her poem,

> Love—is anterior to Life—
> Posterior—to Death—
> Initial of Creation, and
> The Exponent of Earth.

PREPARATION

Lear went down for seven days in early February. He lay on his side and wouldn't get up. That is always a bad sign with elephants. In the wild the others try to lift the sick one up. They lean against him, one on each side, like a pair of elephant crutches. Jo worried over Lear, hand-fed him and dragged a water trough beside him. His wrinkled skin stretched over his legs and broad sides, folds of it hung around his belly. He kept his trunk curled in close to him as if it felt tender. Lear was drained of his great strength and lay with frightened eyes, tended by Jo.

I ordered books from the library but what they had was old: G.H. Evans, *Elephants and their Diseases* (Rangoon, 1910), W. Gilchrist, *A Practical treatise on the treatment of the diseases of the elephant, camel, and horned cattle, with instructions for preserving their efficiency* (Calcutta, 1851), F.A. Rikes, *Elephant Physiology* (Massachusetts, 1968), J.H. Steel, *A manual of the diseases of the elephant and of his management and uses* (Madras, 1885) and a series on their anatomy by L.C. Miall

and F. Greenwood in the *Journal of Anatomy and Physiology* (London, 1877–78). A little more is known today than a century or thirty centuries ago, but not much. What I discovered was what Jo already knew. With most non-mortal diseases, given fluid and sleep, they heal themselves, and with mortal diseases, they die.

When Lear still hadn't got up after three days, Jo went into the Safari office and telephoned Dr. Yu, a veterinarian originally from Burma, who worked in the large animals section at a nearby university. Dr. Yu was a gentle and sad-voiced man. Though elephants were not his specialty, Jo liked him because he had grown up in a country where elephants and people have lived together for centuries, where elephants eat and work in city streets. I had talked to Dr. Yu once to ask him what he knew about elephant infrasound. He said he'd read about it but the old elephant men had never spoken of it. He asked me if I knew an elephant can read a man's thoughts, and then he laughed. He was full of folk talk of elephants. He told me that pregnant women pay money in the city streets to walk under an elephant's belly three times, a charm to protect their babies. Then he added, "That's all superstition, we don't believe in things like that here, do we?"

I was stroking Lear's head when Jo came back from the office. "What did he say?"

"Not much."

"He must have said something."

"He said he didn't know much we could do."

"Did you try anyone else?"

"I left a few messages."

"What did you tell Dr. Yu?"

"I said, 'Lear won't stand up.'"

"And what did he say?"

"He said, 'That's bad.'"

This was the first day that we didn't make love. We sat together with Lear until I had to go. I asked Jo if he wanted me to stay and he said, "No, you've got your mother to look after too."

I left him peeling an orange and feeding it to the elephant bit by bit. His shoulders were slumped forward. He looked as if he were already in mourning. I was annoyed by his resignation. I wondered how anyone could be so arrogant as to give up so quickly. I wondered who had beaten the hope out of him.

———◆———

The next day was a bitter, windy twenty degrees below zero. Jo asked me to keep all the elephants in while he went to see Dr. Yu. The elephants were restive, shuffling together, ears up. Saba was tucked well in under Alice, and Kezia pressed herself against the two of them. Gertrude, who'd been rolling on a tire, stopped and lifted her trunk toward the loft. I was shovelling and hauling dung in a wheelbarrow when I heard a movement in the hayloft and strains of thin harmonica music that rose like an exhalation. I climbed the ladder to look. In the north corner, I could see a strange man leaning against some hay, partly obscured by a wall of bales. I called over, "What are you doing in here? No one's allowed up here."

The stranger twisted his body around without moving his hips. He smiled casually across the tips of his fingers, cupped his harmonica against his chin, and didn't speak. All my senses stood on end as he approached me; I was trying to smell him out, feel him out, the way a woman on an empty street at night listens to quickening footsteps behind her.

The stranger's azure eyes were flecked with grey and his teeth the clean white of someone who doesn't smoke or drink coffee or wine. He wore a felt hat and his leather jacket was the colour of groats. His beard had the bluish tinge of a few days' growth and the hair poking out from under his hat lay in snaky clumps. He stared at me and then averted his gaze with a disarming shrug. He walked loose-hipped over the scattered hay, barely disturbing the dust. I couldn't tell how old he was. There were cocky smile lines at the corners of his eyes. He looked down, assessing me, and when he stepped into the light at the top of the ladder he brought his boots close enough to my fingertips that I slid them back. He squatted down so that his face was too close and I leaned back as far as I dared and froze again. He dropped his harmonica into his breast pocket and flipped open his palm to hand me a little white card embossed with gold. It read:

I am mute.

I stared at him. And then I said, "You're not allowed up here. You'll have to leave. I'm going to call the police. Can you hear?"

He slipped a blue plastic board out of the front pouch of his knapsack. Attached to it was a plastic cover and a writing stick. He wrote on the board and passed it to me, "I play music don't I?"

He took back the board, snapped up the plastic cover and the words disappeared.

"I'm sorry. But you'll have to leave. We have dangerous animals here."

He smiled and wrote, "I am a friend of Jo's."

I leaned in closer to read in the dim upstairs light. As soon as I'd finished, he lifted the screen to erase his words. He smelled of warm leather.

"Does he know you're here?"

The stranger shook his head, turned around the board and wrote, "I didn't tell him I was coming."

He showed me the board, erased and wrote upside down, as quickly as he wrote right side up, "You are very pretty."

I laughed, embarrassed.

He paused and wrote again, "What is the little one's name?"

We both looked down into the barn below where the elephants waited in the hay.

"Saba."

He pursed his lips, frowned and wrote, "That's what you get when you let school kids name your *loxodonta*."

I couldn't help but laugh. I'd heard about the elephant-naming contest. It was a way of getting people to the Safari.

"These elephants are *indicus*. My name's Sophie."

"I know," he wrote.

I waited for him to introduce himself but he didn't.

"What were you playing?"

He smiled, pulled out his harmonica and played a strain of melody. I felt a familiar and welcome shiver inside my stomach. He wrote as quickly right to left as he did forwards.

"Jo told me you liked music."

I made a move to go back down and he wrote quickly and thrust the board at me, "My great-grandmother used to sing it. I don't know the words. Doesn't matter anyway," then he opened his mouth and his head rocked up and down silently as if he were laughing. I thought I could hear air squeezed out between his vocal cords.

I backed down the ladder. He followed me and the elephants turned to us, trunks raised. When Saba came forward, trunk extended in curiosity, he stepped back nervously, arms tight to his ribs, his body arched away from the little elephant. I moved between them and Kezia lifted her trunk innocently to scent him but he ducked backwards and to one side out of her way. None of the others tried to touch him. Lear shifted in his stall and Kezia was fretting, wagging her head back and forth. I could see she was rumbling to the others, the skin on her forehead vibrating. A rough chaos disturbed the barn and I kept myself between the stranger and the elephants. He wandered to the side stalls and craned over the great elephant lying on his side. "What's wrong with Lear?"

"We don't know. He just lay down a few days ago and won't get up. Maybe we should go out front... how do you know his name?"

He looked grave and didn't acknowledge me but kept staring down at Lear.

"I'll help you find Jo," I said.

"Don't bother, he'll find me."

The awkwardness of talking to him was that I couldn't move very far away because I had to read his board. He sauntered along the wall to Jo's corner, familiar with the barn. His back to me, he wrote on his board, "My name's Alecto," and held it up.

He picked up the flashlight beside Jo's cot, flicked it on and off, tested the pillow with the palm of his hand and lifted back the coarse blanket Jo and I had left crumpled there earlier that afternoon. He sank into the sagging mattress, twisted against the wall, pushed his hat away from his eyes, put his boots up on the bed and crossed his ankles. Then he stuck his hand into his pocket, pulled out his harmonica and played that music again, his eyes resting on me, his mouth obscured. I could not tell if he was looking at me or if his gaze was absorbed in something beyond. He played the music of wandering people, unresolved dominants sliding up from his lungs, down from his irretrievable first breath. I should have closed the doors and walked home across the snowy field but I lingered in the barn, pretending to be busy. I liked the feeling of his eyes on me. I knew I should go but my body had different ideas. I warned my body sternly but it kept stirring. It wanted his heat, it wanted to act without conscience, it wanted, and I told it to stop.

———◆———

The next afternoon Jo came into the barns with some horse blankets for Lear.

"Did you see Alecto?"

"Who?"

"Alecto."

"Is he here?"

"Yes, you didn't see him?"

"No. How's Lear?"

"No change . . . I hand-fed him some grain and he drank a little. Isn't Alecto a friend of yours?"

"Is that what he said?"

"No, only that he's known you for a long time."

"Is that so? Help me cover Lear up."

We laid the blankets over his exposed side, stroked his head and his legs, which pushed forward, as if to get up. Elephants breathe poorly lying down because much of their enormous weight rests on a transverse diaphragm. We'd talked about trying to raise him a little and managed to get a few rolled blankets as bolsters under him. They didn't raise him but cushioned his side at least. I was frustrated that we seemed to be doing nothing, but Jo was even terser than usual.

"Why is he mute?"

"Don't know. I heard he was born that way. He's not completely mute."

"Then why does he use that board?"

"Don't know . . . maybe he doesn't like the sound of his own voice."

"Who is he?"

"He does research on elephants—anatomy. His name's Rikes. You showed me some of his articles."

"F.A. Rikes?"

I'd read his autopsy reports. He was an eccentric scholar without affiliations. His reports came out of zoos and safaris abroad. About thirty years ago he'd travelled through Kenya on a killing spree, shooting elephants and doing autopsies on the spot, hunting in a way that would now be impossible. His observations were impeccable and many other scientists drew on the detailed physiology he recorded on that trip. Two decades later, he moved to North America where he did several bizarre experiments. He built a "breathing chamber" with a hose for an elephant to stick its trunk in to measure air volume displacement and learned about breath rate and oxygen transfer. He wrote about the sensory points on the skin of an elephant. In that article he published a map of the elephant's pain centres, marking specific points around the eyes, under the belly, around the shoulders, on the tops of the feet, at the tip of the sensitive trunk. He noted that the research was developed out of the traditional teachings of Indian mahouts. His most recent work was a design for elephant quarters that would eliminate the keeper, a system of hydraulic doors between zoo yards and the barn through which the elephant is enticed with food. He argued that handling elephants is dangerous and that eliminating all human contact is both cheaper and safer in small zoos.

"Why didn't you tell me you knew him."

"Didn't think it mattered. I know most of them one way or another. He's a university man, he doesn't have time for people like me," Jo said contemptuously. "What do I know, I just like being with them. Look, I'm more worried about Lear right now."

I watched as Jo tried to feed Lear and give him something to drink. I stroked the elephant's ears.

"Dr. Yu must have told you something we could do, Jo. What did you talk about?"

Jo clamped his jaw down. "He told me the common problems—infections, heart—but nothing we can fix. There was nothing except a strange folk cure from Burma."

"What was it?"

"We're not in goddamn Burma."

I knew how little Jo would be moved by my words, so I waited in fierce silence until he finally relented. "He said the old elephant men got temple candles, one for every year of the elephant's life, and placed them all around the elephant and burned them until the elephant stood up."

"Let's try it."

"Sophie, I'm just trying to figure out a way of getting him out of the barn when he dies. How do you move a dead elephant? What will we do with the others? I've never lost one before."

"Jo, try, I'll get the candles."

He stopped then because we'd been speaking different languages and he'd finally heard me.

"Do what you want. You will anyway," he grumbled. But I was already on my way out the door and across the field.

When I got to my mother's, Alecto was sitting in my big chair by her bed, talking to her with his blue board. My mother was laughing and she fell silent when I came in. Moore sat on her left shoulder and Alecto was tossing the two Grays sunflower seeds. They flapped playfully in a dry hill of seed husks littered over the carpet at his feet.

Alecto smiled at me, nodded and lifted his fingers in a facsimile of a wave.

"Your friend Dr. Rikes has been keeping me company," said my mother. "Did you know he used to train birds?"

"Have you met before?"

"No," said my mother.

"Yes," nodded Alecto.

"Well that clears that up."

"I know the genus and species if not the individual," she laughed. Her colour was better than it had been for weeks.

Alecto's head flicked back on his shoulders in an exaggerated way with his mouth open in a soundless laugh, like a black mamba snapped up straight, its jaws parted.

"Sunflower seeds aren't good for them," I said, sounding prim even to myself.

He tossed down another one.

I caught my mother's eye and said, "Can I get you a tea?"

It was a joke we'd used for years to get rid of visitors who stayed too long—she'd started it with me when I was a teenager and my friends wouldn't leave. But she just smiled and shook her head and said, "That's fine, Soph. We're fine. I'll let Dr. Rikes here know when I'm tired."

He held up his board to her and then tipped it toward me. "May I have the pleasure of your company for dinner? I do very good order-in."

"Excellent idea," said my mother as I read. "How about Chinese? I haven't had it in ages."

He wrote at the bottom of his board to me, "You too?"

"No thanks." I really wanted to stay. This was the way my mother's house used to feel, full of odd people and ideas, things to discuss and dissect, jokes and people cooking. "I have to go back to the barn. Lear's still not up. Are there any candles? I need lots."

"In the junk drawer."

Alecto looked curiously at me and scribbled, "What for?"

"It's just an idea. There's a phone in the hall when you want to order."

He wrote, "I'll telepath them. First a consult with Eva is necessary!"

My mother laughed. "I can call. I'm partial to moo shu, how about you?"

It would have been so much more amusing to stay. I kissed my mother but she was already turned toward Alecto. He brushed my hand with his and let it stay there as he showed me a list of his favourite Chinese dishes.

When I left the room my mother was up and leading him to the piano. She still played the odd jazz standard though her hands were too stiff for her beloved Beethoven.

"Come now," she said. "What key is that harmonica in? Let's see what you can do."

I listened to them picking their way into "Autumn Leaves" as I fed the birds in the aviary, changed their water and dug through the drawer for my candles. Alecto could improvise, a talent both my mother and I admired. She was singing and changing the tempo on him. I left through the back door reluctantly, matches and candles in a plastic bag, a roll of tinfoil tucked under my arm.

———•◆•———

Jo was still sitting by Lear's head when I slipped into the barn. There were dark blue circles under his eyes and two deep creases across his forehead. He'd slept fitfully all week, rising every few hours to check Lear. He was taking the others out to the yard but not on walks. He'd brought a coffee pot from his trailer to the barn and ate nothing but sandwiches. I quickly shaped nineteen candleholders from squares of foil and placed them in a large circle around the elephant. As I lit the candles, Jo said, "Don't burn the place down."

We sat together, caressing Lear's head and waiting. I had had no sickness with my pregnancy but from the beginning I was exhausted all the time. I fell asleep leaning on Jo and when I woke up the candles were burned down about half way. I opened my eyes and remembered where I was, smelling Jo and the barn, and I said, "Anything?"

"Nothing."

"Maybe they had herbs, or they rang bells, or sang . . . we have no idea. Can you feel his breathing? It's so laboured."

"Their lungs depend on the muscles surrounding them to force the air in and out. Lying on his side like this is making his problem worse."

I knew. Jo kept repeating that over and over. No elephant had ever died in his care. Lear's breath was shallow and his body lay slack. His eyes had lost their panicked look and the lids drooped down. It seemed to me absurd that we hadn't even taken his temperature. He had the lethargy of a fever. But Jo refused. "Why poke around when there's no treatment if he does have a fever," he said.

"Jo, do you think he's really nineteen?"

"That's what it says on his papers . . . I suppose he'd be twenty-one if you counted in gestation."

"I want to try twenty-one."

58

Jo's face softened then, but he shook his head. "Sophie, I've got to get some sleep. I'm falling over. I'm afraid we're going to lose him. Don't leave the candles lit if you think you might fall asleep. Come and get me and I'll take over. Who's taking care of your mother?"

"Alecto was over there when I left. She's been a little better these past few days. She's up and down."

"Better watch him."

"Why?"

"I don't know."

"She seems to like him. He's very sociable."

"I bet."

"Jo, what's he doing here?"

"He wants to do research. They've known him here a long time. He was the one who got them to bring me here."

Before I could ask what kind of research, Jo walked across the barn, dropped onto his cot and slept immediately, like a pebble dropped into a pond.

Alone, I arranged the second set of candles around Lear. I knew no Buddhist scripture and no ceremony and I didn't know what I believed about such things, but I whispered as I lit each candle, "Please, God."

Gertrude was the only elephant in the barn still standing. In the final stillness of the night, she let her head drop and dozed. Afraid to sleep, I stood up and swayed a little. I looked across the stalls at Jo, the moonlight falling through the slats on his face, a man who had chosen to make his home among elephants, to sleep with them, to wake to their morning greeting. His long hair was tousled across his forehead and the worried lines on his forehead slackened in repose. He was the father of my baby. How strange to be here with this stranger in a barn. He was a man who slept on straw, who did not talk much. He knew about elephants, he walked with them and trained them and learned their ways. He tried to fulfil his purpose. In the silence of that barn where everything slept, I looked over at Jo sleeping, Jo whose hands had touched me, Jo who was teaching me to take care of elephants on snow-swept fields, Jo, who tonight had given up hope.

When the candles were half burned down, Lear began to stir. I was standing, leaning on the stall wall, my head dropped and dozing. I snapped awake as Lear raised his head and neck heavily and rumbled out loud, *hrhrhrhrhrhrhr.* He rolled up stiffly from his back hip and shoulder and heaved his great bulk forward for the first time in five days. I was calling to Jo but he was already on his way over. He stepped inside Lear's circle of light and reached his hands out as if to support the elephant, caressing him, welcoming him back, talking, half laughing, disbelieving. I moved back and laughed with relief and watched Jo and Lear greeting each other. The elephant weakly put his trunk around Jo's waist and Jo was already massaging the side Lear had been lying on for so many days. Jo put his forehead to the elephant's trunk and held it there as if he were hugging a small child. Lear's eyes were still heavy with fatigue but an alertness had crept back into his pupils, which reflected the candlelight. I gazed at them and then I stooped down and made my way around them in a circle, extinguishing the fire, picking up the candles, silently thanking the flame beads for each year of life and for those old elephant men who knew a thing or two.

We never talked about the cure. Jo didn't want to admit that it might have worked. In fact, he never liked to admit that any of his elephants fell ill. He preferred to believe they were all immortal, and so was he. The next morning I saw him through my mother's kitchen window walking Lear in the yard outside. When I came back in the early afternoon he was hand-feeding him with warmed grain and water.

Before I could say a word Jo said, "Think you could take Kezia and Gertrude out back by yourself today? I'm going to put Saba and Alice in the yard, and Lear in the big stall. I want to give Lear's stall a good going over."

The day was crisp and bright, the temperatures around freezing. The elephants floated light as milkweed seeds in the sunshine, frisky in the warmth. Jo saw us off.

"Be sure you keep them moving slowly. Walk at Kezia's shoulder. Let her know you're the boss."

We followed the elephant path into the back maples. I'd never been alone outside the yard with them. With Jo we usually kept walking, moving around their sides while they explored the tree branches or the edges of the fencing.

Sometimes we sat down together. I wondered if I dared stop walking, if they'd come to me if I left my place at Kezia's shoulder. We walked past my mother's dark back windows and I waved in case she was looking. And as we moved on, I saw an oak stump big enough to sit inside, smoothed out by animals and wind and water. Its enormous roots spread along the surface of the snow and dipped down under the earth, where they still lived somehow. Weary, I slipped inside.

We were in a small gully, out of the wind, and the sun reflected off the sides of the exposed rocks. I watched the elephants use their trunks to dig around the bottoms of the trees, contented to stop. We all basked in the sun and, drowsing, I thought about my baby. I talked to her aloud and inside my head, too. I told her I was waiting for her and that I loved her already. I told her to hurry up and grow and let me hold her. I told her that I didn't know where we were going or how things would be. I told her I hoped she'd like elephants and carved saints and the smell of strange spices and sitting near campfires at night. I wrapped my barn sweater close around me, smelling of straw and elephants, and curled up in my stump, my body warm and my face cool. As I grew rounder with this baby, I felt all my joints begin to loosen. I felt as if I were talking to this new life all the time, even when I was talking to others. I thought briefly about working the elephants, working myself, keeping us all moving. But I didn't. I watched them dawdling along the fences, using their trunks to move around chunks of ice. Others could do the work today, cleaning barns and dying. Today I had a baby to grow. I dozed and felt the cold on the end of my nose and the warmth in my body where something was beginning, and I thought about seeing an elephant rise and dance with a man in Buddha's light.

KYRIE, ELEISON
(Lord, have mercy)

By the end of February we were having difficulty controlling my mother's pain. We came home from our visits to the hospital and I raged against the doctors. My mother's treatments made her ill. But after the doctors recited the side-effects they didn't want to see her any more.

They had asked her to wait for her treatment on a stretcher in a hallway because all the other rooms were busy. I watched people in street clothes and hospital uniforms hurry by without seeing her as she lay, bald head poking out, bony frame covered with a cotton sheet, another fallen leaf. I watched for two hours, wandering back and forth with magazines she couldn't read. I dragged around her coat and a plastic bag with her boots and her big purse and finally I stuffed them under her stretcher. An orderly hurried over briskly and asked me to move them. Our nights were wakeful now and I was always tired. I turned my back to this officious man and the stretcher in exhaustion and I

shouted at the desk with its high counter, "What the hell is going on here? I want a room!"

My mother pressed her sheet against her chest, sat straight up and snapped loudly at me, "That's enough, Sophie. They treat us. They don't teach us to die. You look like a bag lady with all that stuff, go sit down! I'm fine."

There she sat, her back naked, high up on the stretcher, eyes imperious as a spoiled three-year-old's. The minute she shouted "die" the hallway fell silent and people noticed her enough to turn away. A nurse stood up behind the desk and I dropped the boots while I juggled our coats and bags. Just as the nurse came beside us, my mother caught my eye and started to laugh as if it had all been a joke. Her eyes pleaded with me, "Please laugh too. Laugh with me and get me through this hell. We got our way. They'll move us through now. Please laugh."

"I am going to be a bag lady if you keep throwing your clothes off in public," I said lamely and laughed a little.

"Let me help you with that," said the nurse. "Let's see, we should be able to get you in now Mrs. Walker . . ."

That evening at home, I took out the phone book, looked up "home care" and I hired a nursing agency to send someone to sit with her when I wasn't there in the afternoons. My mother was lying in bed, grey and weak with the sickness of the treatments.

She heard me and called out, "Sophie, what are you doing? I won't have strangers in this house!"

"I need help!"

"I hate strangers in the house. I won't have fussing, pursey-lipped women in my bedroom."

"Well, tell them to stay in the kitchen then."

"I don't need a babysitter," she spat. "If you weren't so busy with your elephant man you'd have more time around here."

But I couldn't do this all alone. Alecto was the only one who came by. He had no fear of her baldness, of her yellowing skin and her changing moods, of her oxygen tank and needles. When she forgot things or struggled with details he nodded agreeably and didn't try to correct her. He made her laugh. He wrote on his board to me when I thanked him for coming so often, "People often desert at the end. They're afraid. I'm not. I've had experience."

He was a perfect visitor. He sat for an hour or so, wrote charming stories, bit by bit, filled in with his own pantomime and questions from my mother. He had refined tastes in music and when she was too tired to talk they sat together listening to recordings of the same piece performed by different artists. My mother loved this. Some days Alecto sat in the corner and played his harmonica. After one of his visits my mother said, "If your father had grown old he might have ended up like your Alecto. They're amusing men to come and go but don't ever marry one."

"How do you know him really?"

"I don't. At least I didn't till he just walked through the door. I thought it was you."

"Weren't you afraid?"

"Why would I be? He wrote he was from the Safari

right away and then he said that he knew you so I thought it was all right."

"You should lock your doors . . . he said he knew you from before."

"I'm sure I haven't met him. He said he met me at the bird barns but I'd remember. How many mutes do you meet in your life?"

"Jo says he can talk. I don't like him walking in."

"It's a question of style. Do you lock your doors?"

Of course not. So I let it go. If he helped her pass the time then he was a welcome visitor.

She amused herself with the revolving door of nurses for whom she had three categories: talkers, tidiers and tea-drinkers. I loved the ones who cooked something for us and left it in the oven. Some of them wouldn't come back because of the birds. That's what they said.

"Are you instructing the budgies to dive at these women?" I asked after three complaints in three days.

She laughed and objected, "I have to survive!"

Her favourite was a woman in her sixties from England called Lottie who came regularly on Tuesdays and Thursdays. She was tiny with large, reddened gardener's hands, wiry grey hair and a straight back. She didn't need to work. The agency told me she only took on palliative cases. The first day Lottie said, "I know you artists, you just want to shock the rest of us."

That pleased my mother.

"Come play chess with me, Lottie," she said.

And the woman answered, "I don't know about such things."

"Well, I'll teach you."

So my mother taught her chess, and when I came in and they put aside the game, my mother said to me, "I whupped her again," and to Lottie, "Now you'll remember me when I die! You'll say, 'That's the one who taught me to play chess.'"

"There! Is that the kind of good teacher you are? And in front of your own daughter! I haven't a competitive bone in my body. Sophie, do you know what this bad woman did today? I said I couldn't stand the smell of the birds and she took out a cigarette and smoked it in bed. How do you like that? Artists! Next time I'm going to get all those birds in their cage and open some windows!"

"It's seven below."

"I don't care a bit. Do her some good."

I wished Lottie could come every day. She had a gentle touch and she liked to cook. She managed to get someone in to clean, and room by room she aired out the house without losing a single budgie. Even Moore would come to her. On the days when my mother was very ill, she sponge-bathed her and sat quietly with her. They planned both their summer gardens together. She left seed catalogues strewn all over the bed, and she was the only one who ever gave me a hug when she left. Lottie always said, "Now you call if it gets too hard and I'll just come along."

When I was by myself, I brought the elephants to the back fence for my mother to see in the afternoons. She stood looking through the kitchen window, waving at all of us. I taught Saba to flick her trunk in a kind of salute. I asked the bird-keepers to come and visit. One of them came once, with some treats for the Grays, and told my mother how well she'd done with them. I brought her art books from the library and new recordings and looked for the old movies she'd always liked. She decided she was going to follow the politics in Quebec in French and ordered French magazines. Then she badgered me to discuss it with her. She asked me to play the recordings of the elephants I was making. When she had a little more energy she worked at a system of labelling and transcribing the sounds. It was painstaking work but she said that listening to their rumbles and infrasound made her feel very calm. It must have been true. I often found her asleep, the tapes run to the end.

One late afternoon as I left the barns, I could hear across the fields Arvo Pärt's *Te Deum*. My mother was playing it full volume at the house, and the swelling chants of the bass voices and double bass, *Tibi omnes angeli, tibi caeli et universae potestates,* throbbed across the silence of the snow-covered rocks. Dusk falls hard and short in winter, and as I approached the house the stiff, rising arpeggios of the hymn of praise drowned out even the loud crunch of my own boots on the dry snow. Staccato strings like bells pierced the gathering dark. I walked slowly, listening, freezing, and I sat on the back porch until I finally heard the men's *Miserere nostri, Domine.* Their deep voices were joined by the soaring violins which gave way to the women's *In te, Domine, speravi,* nudging the music toward its final *amen* and *sanctus.* Through the back door window I could see my mother sitting in the dark kitchen, her elbows on the table, her hands wrapped round a cup of tea, staring into dead air, absorbed in the sound.

Pushing open the door, I mouthed to her, "A little loud!" covering my ears.

"I like it loud. I feel like a slug on the conductor's baton."

Her cheeks were gaunt, as if that very afternoon the disease had eaten her away a little more, shrinking her before my eyes. I stomped the dry snow off my boots and dropped my heavy coat over a chair.

"Can I turn it down?"

She shrugged.

"You had it on so loud I could hear it at the barns."

"Well, I'm sure your elephants would like it. How's Lear?"

"He's all right."

"You'll appreciate Pärt when you get older."

"I already do."

"You won't until you're as old as me."

"Come on! Was Alecto by today?"

"No."

"He hasn't been around for a few days. I wonder where he goes."

"No point wondering … those kind of men never bother telling you."

"Where's Lottie?"

"She had to leave early. I told her to go."

I poured myself a cup of tea and cut off a big slice of store-bought coffee cake. We ate badly in the winter. We survived on eggs and toast, canned beans and soups like two old bachelors. At our last farm, before I'd left home, there'd been a fish man who drove up unexpectedly with his freezer-van full of Boston bluefish and shrimps and rich scallops and occasionally a lobster. My extravagant mother bought bags of it, just because he came door to door, and we feasted for a few nights on rice and seafood. The rest of it sat buried in the freezer getting freezer burn. In the summers we always had sprawling, unkempt gardens with lettuces and tomatoes and bushels of beans. We ate lots of fresh salads. But my mother's freezer was empty this winter. I could see that she hadn't had a garden, and I wondered how long she'd really been ill.

"Want to see something interesting?" I said, devouring my cake.

I pulled some of Saba's sketches out of my knapsack and laid them on the table. Then I went to the front hall closet where I'd been keeping the others. I sorted them and laid them down in the order they'd been done, the one made against me first. It had dark blotches at the beginnings of the lines where Saba had fiddled with her marker before moving it, and the excited scribble over both lines. The last drawing,

72

one Saba had done that afternoon, was spare, just an arc across the top third of the page with a single line intersecting it.

My mother looked at them curiously and lifted up first one, then another. She passed her thin hands over the table and looked some more.

"Who did these?"

"One of the elephants, the baby."

She laid down the page she was holding and picked up the last one.

"It takes a cultured sensibility to appreciate a line," she said critically. "The little genius appears to have a good sense of balance. If one of my students had done these I'd say there was happiness and intention in these lines."

"They remind me of those endless Asian bamboos."

She laughed. "Or de Kooning. . . . What does your elephant man say?"

"His name's Jo."

"What does he say?"

"He hasn't seen them. I just do them with the elephants on my own."

"And Dr. Rikes?"

"He's not interested either. He says it's either random or learned behaviour."

"Well, tut tut, that's safe. What do they know?" My mother turned back to them again curiously. A young budgie flopped on the table and she brushed it off gently. We ate a can of spaghetti together, holding our plates in our hands so we could keep looking at the pictures.

"There's an energy to them. Look at this one," I said, "it comes to a point and crosses the page at a pleasing angle..."

"Do you see how the lines have a pressure and then disappear?"

"... yes, their trunks are as sensitive as a hand. She'd be physically capable of that."

"Do you think she can see them?"

"I don't know ..."

"They don't look like drawings made by someone relating primarily to visual stimulus."

"What would they be then?"

"Maybe movement? I don't know. The strangest part is in the variation of the line thickness, that's done with intent."

We got out some of my mother's big art books and looked at oriental paintings and at the moderns. We put our dishes in the sink and experimented ourselves, with blindfolds, standing above the table with our markers. Her lines were freer than mine. Our papers crinkled and our strokes faltered. It was easier, at first, to do big strokes, like a child stretching out her arm and scribbling.

"Their trunks have a hundred thousand muscles," I complained. "How many do our hands have?" and I tossed my marker on the table.

"I wish I'd known about this when I was teaching," she said, sitting down suddenly. "The students would have loved it. Look what it does to your lines ..."

The small carport attached to the kitchen caught the north wind and sent it howling around the window. Safe inside, warm and tired out, I leaned into the sound of the wind, snow would bury us yet again that night. I tidied our few dishes and glanced at my mother appraising our work and the elephant's. Her eyes were bright, but her skin was dark and drawn.

Abruptly she said, "Did you see the last thing I was working on?"

Her studio, a small uninsulated log outbuilding, was about three hundred metres behind her house, tucked against a hedge that bordered on the Safari fence. She had an old-fashioned oil space-heater in the corner which would heat it up in a few hours, but neither of us had made the effort to go over and get the place warmed up since I'd come home.

"C'mon, we're going out," she said.

"It's late, it's storming."

"To hell with it," she said, "I might die tonight."

"You're not going to die tonight."

We wrapped ourselves in heavy sweaters and socks and I helped her slip on a pair of boots. I pulled a thick wool hat over her bald head and put on my barn toque. I found a flashlight and said, "Wait, I'll shovel a path, we can't go through this snow."

"Christ, Sophie! It's late! I can walk in your tracks."

And so, holding on to the back of my jacket she walked behind me. I made short steps through the drifting snow and moved forward slowly. I heard her voice but I couldn't turn.

"You know, Sophie, everyone says they don't want heroics at the end, but I do."

"What?" I tried to swivel round.

"Don't turn around," she said. "If you stumble, I'll go with you."

"What do you mean, heroics?" I said, turning half forward and taking another step, feeling her mittened hand pinching a big fold of cloth on the back of my coat. She leaned her head toward me and spoke into my ear so her voice wouldn't be blown away by the wind.

"I want enough to keep me out of too much pain but I don't want any overdoses. If I want that I'll do it myself. I'm not afraid of pain. I want the full experience of all this, it'll be my last. I just wish there were some way of getting it down. That's the great waste of it, one of the biggest experiences of your life and you don't get to tell anyone. Can you imagine what people would be able to do?"

"Can we talk about this at home?"

"No, I don't want to. If I change my mind, if the pain is too bad, I'll tell you and you can do it. You'll be able to."

"Do what?"

"I want to die as much as I can by myself. I want to be home. I've got enough morphine stockpiled if we need it. It's in the old medicine box. Soph, I'm glad you're here."

How like her. I want heroics, but only at home. I want painkillers but not too much. I don't want drugs but I might change my mind. I want to die on my own, but you might

76

have to help me. I wanted her to say it would be all right. But she didn't. She was afraid.

The snow was deep and the door of her studio was frozen and I couldn't get it open. I struggled and dug away the snow with my hands, tears freezing on my cheeks, because of course we hadn't thought to bring a shovel. She wasn't a clear person. When I was younger and I used to complain about that, she'd answer, "Why would you want things clear? Life is too complicated." I finally got the snow away from the studio door, pulled it open, and flipped up the electric switch. The large north window was iced, inside and out, with snow blowing from the Safari fields. Even the dust was frozen. She moved past me, turning on the floor lamps and track lights. Then she hurried back and switched off the bare bulb inside the door. The walls were hung with familiar canvases, things I'd seen before, large oils from her last sketching trip up the Labrador coast, a winter wolf nosing around a garbage dump and one of her icebergs in purples and pinks and blues still not finished. Strewn throughout the studio were tiny sweaters, dozens and dozens of shrunken, misshapen, cut up and partly unravelled sweaters. I could see our entire history in sweaters: my baby sweaters, my toddler pullovers, my little girl pink angoras, my red matched set, my teenaged tight-ribbed bodysuits, a favourite oversized beige and brown herringbone that I'd always worn on our camping trips. Hers were there too: her black sweater with the pearl buttons, her Irish knit, her paint-flecked work sweaters, the one with the enormous turtleneck that folded down like a necklace. There were dozens more that I didn't recognize: men's cardigans, boys' hockey sweaters, children's sweater coats with patterns of figure-skating girls and little Scottie dogs, women's cocktail capes, grannies' shawls, doll sweaters. She had shrunk them all, and those that didn't shrink she'd cut down. She'd chosen them from a clothesline strung at odd angles, rows and rows of discarded sweaters she'd shrunk and hung up with pegs.

On the south wall she had completed an enormous canvas. She had mounted about four dozen of the smallest sweaters in an astonishing collage. Each arm was placed at a different angle, some open, some closed, and the total effect was of a crowd of children who had danced wildly beyond the sun's governance, shedding their clothes like unnecessary shadows.

I moved up closer to look at the detail of the canvas. She had sewn into some of the buttonholes and collars the tiny feathers of her budgies. She'd drawn bird and animal tracks in the background. She'd woven around these in fine, fine script all sorts of words: *I have toil'd, and till'd, and sweaten in the sun; I could not sweate out from my hart that bitternes of sorrow; sweat the sail taut; She seeketh wool, and flax, and worketh willingly with her hands; sweat gold; labour and drudge, sweatie Reaper; It is no little thing to make Mine eyes to sweat compassion; sweater: one who sweats.*

But when I stepped back I could not see the words any more, so skilfully had she camouflaged them in the textures

78

of the background. She'd selected each sweater not only for its uniqueness—buttons, collars, design, bands—but also for how it had shrunk. Some had shrunk perfectly evenly, coming out as gnomes' clothes. Others had shrunk more along certain wools than others, pulling and straining at themselves, creating new patterns. None of her wildlife painting ever had the shimmering will of this work.

"I love this," was all I could say.

"I know," she said, gazing at her canvas as if it were a stranger. "It works, doesn't it?"

"Why don't you have it over at the house?"

"I never got it framed—it's so big. I wanted to do a box frame."

"That would be perfect. Let's do it. Let's put it in your room. I love the budgie feathers. How many sweaters have you shrunk in here?"

"A couple of hundred. It took me a whole year to get each one to shrink the way I wanted. I can shrink anything now. That little one in the middle I shrunk seven times. Do you know it was a man's sweater?"

"Did you ever show it to the gallery?"

"Yes, they came out and loved it and wanted to take it right away. I didn't want to sell it though. When I wouldn't let them they brought some people out. But it all happened just when they found the first cyst. Anyway, I wanted to keep it for you. I didn't know if I'd ever be able to do another."

She'd shed her skin and come out raw and new. She had

worked very, very hard to go so deep and come back with these images. She mocked and honoured all at once. She made the ruined beautiful, the common haunting. She'd found the passion that might have driven her into years of new work. I wandered into the corner to look at her sketch pads. There were dozens of sketches with fresh ideas.

"What happened, Mom?"

She smiled and sat down on a pile of old newspaper. "I don't know, I really don't. I shrunk one of my own sweaters by accident one day and when I looked at it dry and mis-shapen I liked it. I think I was suddenly open enough to just play again." She hesitated, then finished, "That's why all this is so hard for me, Sophie. I'm not ready. I had more to do. Much more to live. This is not a natural death and I am not ready. I can admit that to you."

There were no words and I went to her and we held each other in that freezing studio underneath her *Sweaters*. She was slowly stripping me bare with all her daily banter about dying, but that was the only time she ever spoke of death. It felt as if she'd reached inside me and pinched closed my blood flow, and as I held her she said quietly, "I know you're pregnant. I hope your baby is as beautiful as you are. Make sure you have time to work, too. There are lots of paintings to sell to help you out. When I die they'll be worth more. They're in that big cupboard at the back. I'm leaving everything to you and your baby."

I could barely hear but the words lodged inside anyway.

Outside she stood a moment looking at the sky and pointed to Cassiopeia and Sirius as she always did. We started back toward the lights of the house and she complained about the cold and the deep snow and chanted with frozen lips, "Men moil and toil for midnight gold ... I can't goddamn breathe!"

"Well, stop talking then!"

We laboured across the back, the wind cutting through us, fresh, heavy snow drifted across the kitchen door. She laughed at me as I jerked it open and said, "Don't let Moore out!"

I certainly hoped Moore wasn't lurking around ready to escape because then, on top of everything else, I'd be running through a snowstorm in the dark searching for an insolent, freezing budgie. When you watch someone dying, you get into the habit of stepping outside yourself. You laugh at yourself doing absurd daily things, heave in the fresh outside air when you can. But by the sick-bed you slow down and listen carefully and try to make the little things comfortable. You even enjoy the routines, because you can't bear too much of the other.

———◆———

When Jo wasn't there, Alecto appeared in the barn and sometimes did the mucking out for me while I sat on a bale of hay, leaned back and put up my feet. I drifted, tired, through days that seemed endless and weeks that disappeared like snowflakes on the palm of my hand. I slept lightly, listening for my mother. The adamantine chains of night pain rattled in the early mornings as the morphine wore off and she'd cry out in her sleep, *please do something,* and wake up. We nursed mugs of tea together waiting for that moment between night and dawn. Only then she'd say, weak and exhausted, "All right now, Soph, I'll take my pill and then let's get a few more hours," as if I were sick too. With the first streaks of winter sun I fell back into my bed separated by a wall from her and slept the greedy sleep of pregnancy until ten, when it was time to get up and feed the Grays and sit with my mother and get ready for the afternoon nurse and go to the Safari.

Jo was renting three of the elephants to a Russian circus that performed through southern Ontario and upper New York State for seven weeks. He was back and forth with Lear and Gertrude. He'd given over some of the daily care of the others to me, watching Kezia and training Saba, who he hoped to bring along with Alice to the later shows. I still hadn't told him I was pregnant although I suppose if he'd wanted to notice he would have. When he was home he came and found me every afternoon. We climbed up into the loft together and made love and lay talking.

"I don't like Kezia being out too long in the cold."

"Don't worry, Jo. I won't keep her out long."

"Make sure you work Saba at least once in the day, and that she listens. This is a point where she still thinks she can get away with not listening."

"All right."

"Remember the enriched grain mix for Kezia."

"I can manage." I pressed against him and smelled his breath.

"I don't like Alecto in the barn so much."

"You're jealous!" I laughed and leaned up on one elbow in surprise. His body stiffened and he pulled back angrily.

"You don't see. He seems to do nothing. But stirring things up pleases him. I've seen it."

"C'mon, Jo."

"Did he tell you he got tossed by a big male? Did he tell you that? He has no feel for elephants. He broke three ribs and his wrist and if he hadn't rolled, he would have got stamped on. He shouldn't be around them. He's arrogant and afraid and they know it. I don't like the feeling in the barn when he's here."

"But why does he keep working with them, then?"

"His nature. He wants and wants, never mind the doing or suffering. He gets others to do the handling and applauds them and makes them feel smart." Jo took my hand. "You have to be humble to be with an elephant. Alecto doesn't have it in him. He likes the idea of the elephants more than the humility it takes to be among them."

"That's why so much of his work is from autopsies?"

"He's always done that, from the days of his killing sprees in Africa. He showed me his diaries. They'd kill and dissect a few a week. He tells about watching one die slowly while he drinks a cup of tea. He notes in that false professor way

83

of his that it seemed to be crying real tears. He should get out of the business. The elephants sense his fear. They'll kill him some day, and I don't want it to be in my barn."

I listened and then I told Jo I'd do everything as if he were there. I didn't believe him. I thought he was being too dramatic. I liked my jealousy theory better.

———◆———

During our barn chores, Alecto taught me about elephant physiology. He showed me sketches of the development of Kezia's fetus. He made diagrams of how their lungs and respiratory systems worked, their digestive systems, their circulation, and how they cooled themselves with their great flapping ears. He showed me how an elephant hears, and made up a theory about the physiology of their infrasound. One day I showed him what I had recorded of their language and played him some samples. He looked at my notes and listened to my tapes with covetous interest. He asked me to replay things and compared my transcriptions with the sounds. Finally he looked up and wrote, "I'm envious!"

"Why?" I said, flattered.

"I didn't know how much language they have."

"You don't spend enough time around them," I teased.

He shrugged. Then he wrote, "Have you ever heard an elephant laugh?"

"I don't know," I said. "Sometimes they look as if they're laughing."

"But is there an articulation?"

"I don't know."

"I know where their tickle spot is."

"What do you mean?"

"A tickle spot, on the belly, close to the mammaries." He erased and wrote upside down, "Get your recorder. Let's see if they laugh."

Intrigued, I went to Jo's corner, pulled out the recorder and the boom mike. I put it together and took it into the stall area and said to Alecto, "You tickle and I'll record."

Alecto shook his head and gestured that he'd hold the mike.

"It's only Alice and Saba," I said, as Saba fiddled with the tape-recorder. "Saba, back."

Alecto held up his board for me to read. "Run your ankus very lightly back and forth over the belly here." He made a sketch and marked a point just behind her front foreleg.

"All right, hold the boom as close to her forehead as you can," I said, handing it to him across the stall wall.

Lightly I ran my ankus over the spot Alecto had shown me. Alice shifted aside and dropped her trunk to brush it away. I asked her to stand and I kept close to her and tickled her again. I couldn't hear anything, but her physical reaction to the touch was again to move away. I asked her to stand again and she did. I heard the door open and turned to see Jo coming in from the transport trailers.

"What the hell are you doing?"

Neither of us answered. Jo walked over to Alecto, took the boom from him and ripped down the mike. He switched off the recorder and snarled, "Get out of here."

Alecto looked at me, shrugged as if to say, *What's gotten into him?* He put on his jacket and left.

I went over to Jo and said, "We were only trying to record what sounds she'd make if I touched her tickle spot."

"Tickle spot!"

"Alecto showed me."

"You believe everything he says? And what the hell were you using your ankus for?"

"Well is there one?"

"Why do you think they like to roll around on the tires?"

I stayed silent. Jo drew himself up straight, the way he did when he was working on a difficult training move, and said, "Sophie, you can only record their normal behaviour. Nothing else."

"Who do you think you're talking to?"

"My barn. My elephants."

"Why do you hate Alecto so much?"

"You used the stand command on Alice to force her into something there was no reason to be doing. She can't comprehend that. It's like lying to her. I don't want you doing things like that. I don't want any accidents in here and I don't want you getting hurt. If Alecto has to be in here, I want you to keep him away from them."

"He never goes near them if he can help it."

"He tries to do it through you."

I did play back the recording of Alice's laugh. It was a variation of the sound she made sometimes when she shimmied a tire into place to roll on. At first there was a little sigh of pleasure, but as I'd continued to touch her and ask her to stand for me there was a strained rumble and a sharp intake of breath and another uncomfortable rumble, the way a child held and tickled begins giggling and ends crying and pleading to be let go.

ELEPHANT-ENGLISH
DICTIONARY
PART TWO

Empathics

Empathics are a continuous thread running through Elephant; the term refers to what in human discourse we identify as human emotion: happiness, grief, anger, joy, contentment, melancholy.

Whereas the Platonic tradition elevates reason over the emotions, the Elephant world-view is closer to Wittgenstein's, with an emphasis on the correlation between reality and language. Possessing a language expands the intellect and extends the will. Thought alone cannot breathe life into the signs of language, what can is the use of these signs in the stream of life.

A Note on Rhythm

The wonderfully lyric composition of everyday Elephant is characterized by creative play with rhythm. I suspect that my Safari elephants, taking advantage of their extensive leisure time, have amused themselves by developing a repertoire of complex metrics. Mature elephants breathe about twelve times per minute when not speaking. This is a rate similar to humans and so I have not hesitated to borrow the formal rhythms of English, which were originally borrowed from Latin, and entrenched in the language with the translation of the Book of Common Prayer. H.W. Fowler in his *Modern English Usage* writes that a passage is rhythmical when "it falls naturally into groups of words each well fitted by its length & intonation for its place in the whole & its relation to its neighbours." By this definition, most of Elephant is rhythmical.

I suspect that rhythm and the frequent recurrence of the empathics are the two main organizing principles of the Elephant language, and the backbone of Elephant grammar.

Most common feet in Elephant prosody

Anapest	(short—short—long)
Dactyl	(long–short–short)
Iamb	(short—long)
Proceleusmatic	(short—short—short—short)
Spondee	(long—long)
Tribrach	(short—short—short)
Trochee	(long—short)

There are certain features of rhythm that transcend linguistic differences, and I would venture that repetition is one of them. Repetition in any language creates rhythm and the same is true for Elephant, which uses a good deal of repetition. Again I refer the reader to Fowler and the following passage which he chooses as a masterpiece of rhythm:

> And the king was much moved, & went up to the chamber over the gate & wept: & as he went, thus he said: O my son Absalom, my son, my son Absalom! Would God I had died for thee, O Absalom, my son, my son!

^oooor: (13 Hz.) A chant to keep the spirits up, a song of general optimism.

One of the greatest differences between Elephant culture and human culture is Elephant's understanding that happiness is possible when each elephant in a group seeks to achieve not only her own individual purpose but also the purpose of the group. The two happinesses are as deeply and inextricably intertwined as language and thought.

I first heard an instance of this chant when Alice had a contagious parasite and I moved her to a barn on the other side of the Safari. As I chained and closed the door, she called out woefully. But when I came back a few hours later, she was chanting ^oooor and industriously pulling clover out of the bales I'd left within her long reach. There seems to be a powerful impulse in Elephant to simply get on with things. Alice's chant was a variety of "away, melancholy" or "I will praise with my whole heart and show forth all marvelous works."

una una na na na: (15 Hz.) An expression of fatigue,
usually at the end of a day of duty work.

I have often heard Gertrude, Alice and Kezia chanting
this on the way back to the barns after giving children their
elephant rides. It is an expression that seeks meaning in the
most mundane, rejects the distractions of mortality and is
firmly rooted in the present. I think of Stevie Smith's
"Mother, Among the Dustbins."

Mother, among the dustbins and the manure
I feel the measure of my humanity, an allure
As of the presence of God. I am sure
In the dustbins, in the manure, in the cat at play
Is the presence of God, in a sure way
He moves there. Mother, what do you say?

*ooo~erh^: (22 Hz.) A support song, encouraging
another (or oneself) in any difficult task.

When one of our elephants was very young she slipped
down the muddy banks of the pond and into the freezing
water in early spring. Three females immediately started to
help rescue her, tugging and pushing and finally placing
large stones under her front feet to help her get some traction. As they grunted, they rumbled this song, each of them
urging the others on.

nrrrarrr: (20-30 Hz.) Low, repeating, forlorn keening
after a death.

This is chanted with a group. The nearest human equivalent would be holding one's body, rocking, weeping, wailing or keening, depending on the culture one comes from. *(See also *onrrrarrr.)*

*onrrrarrr: (20-30 Hz.) Mourning.

This chant is uttered by one elephant and is commonly combined with a group response *(see nrrrarrr)*. Communal mourning is very important to Elephant harmony, and this rumble functions as a responsive chant, as when a minister says, *May peace be with you* and the congregation answers, *And also with you.*

onr: (35+ Hz.) Comfort.

This utterance is different from **onrrrarrr* because it is uttered audibly. It was one of the first empathics I discovered. Kezia chanted it to me when I was feeling defeated by my mother's illness. It may be an utterance she created for me; I have never heard her use it with other elephants. I include it because it shows Kezia reaching out to a different species. She accompanied the utterance with a caress of her trunk.

When the early Christians called the elephant the "Bearer of all Infirmities" they may have been describing this creative ability to communicate in comforting ways that even humans can understand.

*ma^ohmn: (35+ Hz.) A dream word.

When I was most preoccupied with the final compiling and writing of this dictionary, I dreamed frequently of Elephant, both audible and inaudible. One night I dreamed this word, *ma^ohmn*. In the dream Kezia was standing in the water of a northern lake, paunsing, inviting me to ride inside her. At the risk of offending the logically minded, although I have not been able to find this utterance on any of my tapes I include it here, because, as Blake suggests, the physical senses are only one part of perception.

The Eye of Man a little narrow orb closd up & dark
Scarcely beholding the great light conversing with the
      Void
The Ear, a little shell in small volutions shutting out
All melodies & comprehending only Discord and
      Harmony....
Can such an Eye judge of the stars? & looking thro its
      tubes
Measure the sunny rays that point their spears on
      Udanadan
Can such an Ear filld with the vapours of the yawning
      pit.
Judge of the pure melodious harp struck by a hand
      divine?

rrr~rrr: (20-37 Hz.) Akin to a cat's purring, an expression of profound contentment.

It is difficult to translate the nature of this contentment, which is very infrequent in human discourse. The best I can think of are the sounds a baby makes when nursing, or the sounds small children make (*arum, arum*) while sucking, chewing, tasting or mucking in something delicious.

oo oo oo ooo o o: (4-12 Hz.) A melancholia song.

This song was collected not from my Ontario Safari elephants but from a much abused elephant who lodged with us for several weeks. She was unpredictable, unruly and destructive. I recorded her several times at night and found her chanting this emotional song all alone. It communicates deep resources of something I can only describe as a life-will in the face of her horrible captivity. It reminds me of the blues chant of an anonymous woman who sings with Big Bill Broonzy, a woman whose song came from gospel choirs, tenant farms and slavery.

Amusingly, after the elephant was taken away, I recorded young Saba chanting a variation of *oo oo oo ooo o o* with a common fatigue song *(see una)*. I suppose this might be an example of a kind of world-beat Elephant song emerging and certainly shows the constant and creative transformation of language.

nnn~praonr~nnn: (10 Hz.) A solitude song.

Kezia sings this long chant, in the middle of the night, when all the others are asleep. It is the deepest of rumbles, usually spondaic, and often ends with a terminal flourish *(see wuh)*. It expresses the melancholic pleasures and responsibilities of being last awake in a place wrapped in sleep. I think of Louise Bogan's sleeping furies

> And now I may look upon you
> Having once met your eyes. You lie in sleep and
> forget me.
> Alone and strong in my peace, I look upon you
> in yours.

wuh: (18-20 Hz.) Rest.

This is the last sound uttered before dropping off to sleep. I have also heard young elephants utter this sound when they finally complete a difficult task. It is a single, arrhythmic utterance, a crossing into stillness.

aaaaaaaaa: (lowest possible range, 0-4 Hz.) Empathetic understanding, acceptance in the community.

This is an utterance made at the lowest end of discernible vibrations. It is a sound more intuited than heard. When one elephant chants *aaaaaaaaa* to another, it is expressing its profoundest acceptance, archaic and full of promise.

BREAKING an ELEPHANT

Saba was the first elephant I ever broke.

In India wild elephants are lured in from the forests by tame elephants. Once they're brought back to a human compound they're bound, back legs together, front legs splayed, to trees or posts. Their trunks are tied down. They're neither fed nor watered for a few days. Elephant men badger them with chants and talk, and they're touched all over with branches and sticks. When they grow quieter the men approach and slap their sides, legs, heads, trunks with their hands. If they're calm they're fed a little and the men keep slapping and chanting. If they're not calm they're starved again. This goes on and on until the animal submits. To the human voice. To the human touch. This is what horse people would call "green broke" and it takes a few weeks.

Then begins the long training, to move forward, backward, to kneel and stand, to carry loads, to wear a harness, to do work, to live with humans in their community. "Full broke" is when the elephant acquires a new purpose.

The mystery is that no living creature is predictable. Anything has wild in it and anything can go wild again.

The only tool an elephant-keeper carries is an ankus, which has a history as exotic as the story of domesticating the great animals. The nineteenth-century ankus tells tales of colonialism—one with a hollowed-out place for a concealed flask, one with a built-in knife sheath. I have seen a collapsible ankus designed to fit into a memsahib's headband. I've seen a rough ankus fashioned from the broken haft of a harpoon. I've seen them made of polished steel, pernambuco, and ivory carved with erotic reliefs. I've seen pictures of the gold ceremonial ankus used by King Ianmeiaya to break the virgin women in his Burmese court. I've read about a stained ankus cut from the tree Christ bore on the *Via Dolorosa,* with inlaid mother-of-pearl, fourteen Stations of the Cross and three views of Calvary.

My own ankus is a simple thing, about eighteen inches long like a rider's crop, with a metal hook at the bottom. Jo taught me how to carry it and to use it with respect. He said, "I've seen elephants use sticks to scratch, to dig, to knock things out of trees. But I've never seen an elephant use a stick to hit or prod another creature."

Saba was born in captivity so she was green broke quite easily. Alice taught her to accept us and to accept our touch. Saba watched us working the other elephants and learned our simple voice commands. When she began to eat solid food, Alice taught her to take grain and hay, but we brought her treats—oranges and grapes and ice.

Jo showed me how to work with ideas elephants have themselves. Saba was curious about balls and Jo taught her to play catch with him.

"You have to get rid of the idea that they play ball to please you," said Jo one day as we worked with Saba. "She'll kneel to please you, but even if she wanted to she couldn't really play ball to please you. She plays ball because she loves to, the same way she loves to toss dirt over her shoulders, or reach and grab for leaves in the trees. The best ball-playing comes from loving to play ball, not wanting to please us."

I thought of my early art lessons as a child. I had wanted to please my mother, to be like her, and after every stroke I'd looked over my shoulder to see if she approved. My work was competent, but after I got away from home and started mucking around with sculpture and oils and collage I discovered that I loved doing it whether she was looking or not. Everyone steals ideas and techniques. Watching Saba snag balls Jo tossed just out of reach and toss them back with perfect accuracy, I understood that Saba got ideas from Jo but how well she played ball had nothing to do with wanting to please Jo and everything to do with her own passion.

The most difficult moment in Saba's training was the first day I hung two small sacks of sand over her back to get her used to the idea of weight. She kept flinging them off. I had to shackle her and tie her trunk. It was the first time I'd ever feared her strength. Until then I'd always wanted her near me. Her eyes looked at me as if I'd gone mad. Neither of us liked what was happening and neither of us understood why we were doing this.

Jo said, "If you are unclear, she will be too."

Everyone is unclear sometimes while learning to live with their elephants. After that the harmony of discipline sets in.

Our interest in what we were doing together became our passion. I asked her to admit me, to be respected by me, to be my passion. Many animal trainers think love is irrelevant to their work. Not many think passion is. It is a difficulty of language. Elephants have no word for love. I think getting close to your gods means trust, interest and passion. Some people call this faith. I call it being broken.

Living with elephants broke me.

———◆———

My mother and I were sitting in her bedroom watching television when we heard a knock on the door. Evening visitors were so rare that she said, "Don't bother going, it's probably Bible-thumpers."

I got up to look and when I opened the door, there stood Alecto.

"I'm surprised you didn't just walk in," I said.

He pulled his slate out of his pocket and wrote, "I tried to. It was locked."

"Do you want to come in?"

"I want you to come out."

I shook my head and said quietly, "I don't go out in the evenings."

"She won't mind."

My mother called from the bedroom, "Who's at the door?" Alecto walked past me into the house.

"Well, Dr. Rikes, it's late, but come in, come in." My mother sat up and pointed to the chair I had been sitting in.

Alecto always knelt for a moment beside her bed, taking her hand and smoothing it with his own while he held her eyes in his. My mother called it his mute trick.

"He can't walk in and say, 'Nice day,' or 'How the hell are you?'" she said, "so he connects that way. It's melodramatic, but so is he."

He got up and sat in my chair and didn't take off his coat. He wrote on his slate, "I need to borrow your daughter."

She read, showed me and said to him, "Well, ask her, then."

Before he could finish writing on his slate I said, "I'm not going out. It's late."

"I don't mind, Sophie," said my mother, "if that's what you're worried about."

"I'm not. Tea?" I said.

She laughed and said, "Go on, Sophie, I'll be fine for a few hours."

He held out his slate. "I just wanted to ask you about some new research."

My mother turned up the volume on the TV and said,

"Do you both good to get out of the sick room. I'll be here tomorrow, I hope. You come in the afternoon, Dr. Rikes, I'll receive you in bed."

He nodded in his parody of a laugh and I frowned at her.

Alecto's truck was in the driveway where the snow was piled high. I hadn't had time to shovel and Lottie and the other nurses had been parking on the road since the snows had got so deep. Alecto's four-wheel drive lifted us over the snow and he backed out onto the long country road toward Highway 6. He flipped on the radio and I didn't talk because he couldn't write and drive at the same time.

He pulled up to a hotel called The Coronation at the corner of the highway and Safari Road. We jumped down from the warm truck into that peculiar bite of late-night cold. We pushed through the door and the tangles of our own frozen breath, stamping our feet, shedding our coats in the overheated, stale air. There are two kinds of drinking in these small hotel bars—the quick drink of a pass-the-evening traveller and the long reiterating drink of the local regular. We took a small pedestal table with a couple of wooden chairs, and before we were settled a skinny waitress in tight jeans and a red ribbed sweater dropped a pitcher of draft and two slim draft glasses on the table.

"I guess we're having draft," I said.

"He always does," she answered, nodding toward Alecto. "You want something different?"

I shook my head, Alecto handed her some bills and she didn't bother to make change. The place was coated with a film of smoke and the smell of stale beer, the kind of place where toilet doors don't stay closed and the graffiti in the stalls is scratched in. I'd had my first sip of beer, heard my first country and western band, played my first game of shuffleboard in a bar like this. When I was younger I never left hotel bars until they turned the lights on.

Alecto held up his glass briefly heavenward and scribbled quickly, "Cheers, to our first drink together, and to the decor."

I held up my glass and drank too.

"Isn't it cold. It's a bit obscene to bring tropical animals to a climate like this, isn't it?"

Barroom banter has an insistent pace that was slowed by Alecto writing. I settled in for a little debate, tossing out the subject like a bowl of peanuts with the beer.

"No more obscene than you visiting the arctic," he wrote.

"And being put on display?"

He shifted happily. "The animals make do, they have leisure, an easy life."

"They make do. They have no choice."

"Who has choice? If you had a choice wouldn't you be in Africa? Is duty a choice?"

Point.

"But I came out of love."

"And what is the love that brought you, duty or choice?"

I paused. Both? Neither?

"I don't know, but the fact is animals have no choice once they're put in these places. They get depressed or they get domesticated."

It was fertile ground for a good drinking night. Animal rights. Animal intelligence.

"Do you think if they could talk it would make a difference?"

He stared at me, challenging, a dangerous debater, not afraid to use my discomfort with his muteness to win, not afraid to use anything to win. I decided not to temper myself tonight. If my advantage was my voice, I'd use it.

"It was the serpent's speech that tempted Eve, much more than the fruit. And it wasn't what the serpent said but that he could talk at all. She was amazed by his ability to talk. If animals spoke we might be tempted to many things."

He smiled and wrote, "So it was speech, not knowledge, that led to the Fall?"

"It was animal speech that led to knowledge and freedom."

"And it caused the Fall?"

"It led to knowledge."

"And freedom?"

"Fallen freedom. 'Without choice, what profits inward freedom?'"

"God has perfect knowledge, therefore perfect prescience. If he knew what would happen why did he allow the serpent speech?"

It was a dance we'd both danced before and we enjoyed it. Banter, cheap talk of rights and freedoms, providence, foreknowledge absolute. I enjoyed reading his side. It made me feel quicker, smarter.

Alecto drank fast. I thought of my baby and slowed down. The waitress picked up our pitcher, expertly dripped its last drops into each of our glasses and dropped down another. I went to the washroom, where two young girls putting on mascara were joking about some men at the bar. "I know all of them," one girl said. "And only half of them's worth knowing." I wandered back up through the smoke and felt Alecto appraising me across the gloomy room. When I sat down I said, "Alecto, where are you from?"

"The south. You?"

"From around here. How do you know Jo?"

"We met at a zoo years ago. Didn't he tell you?" He watched my eyes, peeled off his board and continued, "Jo was the only one who could get elephants to do what I wanted."

"What did you want?"

"I was researching sensory points. I had an old map from India made by the mahouts."

"I read that article."

His bright eyes caught mine, looking to see if I was mocking him, and reassured, he continued writing. "No zoo would give me access. Jo was in a Florida petting park and all he wanted to do was take care of elephants in a decent place like this. I told him I could arrange this job if he'd help me do my experiment."

"And he did it."

Alecto nodded.

"What did you do?"

"Jo kept the elephant down. I beat the sensitive spots and recorded the pulse and external reactions."

"How did he keep him down while you were hitting him?"

"Voice commands."

"That must have been an amazing elephant."

"Amazing keeper."

"I don't see what kind of evidence you were looking for when you already had the map."

"I wanted to see for myself. Refine the chart."

"What for?"

He looked down at his glass, then wrote quickly, "It was a long time ago."

"I've read your physiology articles too—you've killed a lot of elephants."

"I was a good shot. I usually could get them with one bullet through the brain. There weren't so many tourists in those days. The villagers lined up to help to get the meat. It was fascinating—I did all ages, both sexes. You'd never get permission to do that kind of study now. Everyone uses my studies. Even the vet schools."

I shook my head and watched him studying my face. He took my hands, the way he took my mother's hands, and tried to look into my eyes. I didn't like the feeling but out of shame I didn't pull away. He turned my hands palms down on the table, covered them both with one hand and wrote with the other, "I never noticed how beautiful your forearms are."

I laughed. There is no new language.

He looked at me, his lips turned up ironically, his eyes angry. "Why is it all the words seem to have been said before?"

"They haven't. Why is it we think in clichés? Why is it we think it should always feel like the first time?"

He shrugged and let me go.

"What did you want to talk about?"

"Maybe you won't like it." His knuckles were clenched white on his pen and he wrote from injured merit.

I waited.

"I need your help. If Kezia's baby dies, or is born dead, I want to do an autopsy. The Safari says I can, but only if Jo agrees. They say it's his baby. I need you to help me persuade him."

"If Jo doesn't want it, I can't do a thing."

His body was tight with anger, still. "You underestimate your influence."

"Believe me, I don't. Why doesn't Jo want it?"

"He thinks it's bad luck," he wrote glibly.

"What makes you think it won't survive? Jo's never said that."

"The odds are against her. There aren't many live births in captivity."

"You've already done this kind of autopsy. I remember reading about it."

"That's what Jo said."

"I don't know." I was tempted. It would be an interesting thing to see.

He leaned forward charmingly, his jaw still stiff, and wrote, "No need to answer now, just keep it in the back of your mind."

I erased his slate and said that I thought I should be going. The beer was making me feel tipsy and I shouldn't have been drinking anyway with my baby. I wanted to get home before he said anything else. I shouldn't have let his hands linger on my arm. I shouldn't have enjoyed the touch. I shouldn't have laughed at him. Nothing had happened. But I still wanted to get home. I should have known that even though nothing had happened, something had.

The sicker my mother got the more I wanted from her. I pulled out boxes of old photographs to get her to tell me our story. The boxes were a jumble of three generations of family, dozens of my mother's friends, places I'd never seen, my old school pictures, holidays and sketching trips we'd taken. We sat sorting and talking and she took up handfuls of my baby pictures and said, "Look at you, you were such a gorgeous baby, it was like falling in love, Soph."

There were dozens of snapshots of me growing up. She didn't like posed pictures. I was usually dirty, mucking in her paints, digging in her gardens, arms wrapped around our various dogs and cats, holding out frogs and snakes and grasshoppers.

"Why aren't there any pictures of me dressed up?" I laughed.

"You never were," she said. "You loved these outfits, skirts with ruffles and rubber boots. You put them together and that's what you'd wear."

There were pictures of her at her openings, with red fingernails and bright red lips. She favoured tight cocktail dresses that pushed up her small breasts and nipped in her waist. There was only one picture of her working. She wore her hair pulled back and a blue apron covered with small flowers over her trousers. I was already older than she was in those photos. How young she did everything. As if she knew.

There were no pictures at all of some of the things I remembered, of her sitting smoking on the porch for hours when the critics tore through her shows, of her when her own mother died, of her when my father came for his only visit then left again, of her wandering through the house the day we heard he died in a car crash when I was still a child, drunk with another painter, smashed against a linden tree, across the ocean.

She met my father in France where she'd gone as a student. I fingered the half dozen photographs of my mother and father in Paris, my mother with her arm around a statue of Montaigne, his lips painted red by the students, my father smoking in a café, shot through a steamy window, my mother sketching with him at the caves of Lascaux.

"Why didn't you stay together?"

My mother left him when I was eighteen months old. I hoped there might be a few new details in those cardboard boxes, in the stories I'd heard before. She'd left and my father had tried to follow her to Canada and live with her. My only memory of him was from that visit. I was about two years old and he gave me an ice cream cone. I bit into it and screamed with the fiery shock of cold in my head. I wasn't sure if I remembered or if the story was family lore. He was a dark, laughing man, clowning for the camera, someone I would have liked to have known. They touched in every photo. There was a picture of him towering over the little Austin he'd bought when he arrived in Montreal. They took drawing trips together in the little car, slept in northern motels and drank in barrooms with signs that read Ladies and Escorts. There was a picture of my young mother sitting on his shoulders under one of those signs. Her hands were thrust up in the air exuberantly, but she was very thin.

"Where was I?"

"You were sitting by our feet," she explained. "I was exhausted and he wanted to take pictures outside bars and go drinking. I used to wash your diapers in the hotel sinks at night and dry them by hanging them out the windows of the car."

She reached over and took the photographs from me and handed me some of my baby pictures. "When I first got pregnant with you I cried and cried. One of his old lovers came to me, a lanky girl with black hair, and she said, 'But why don't you accept, men have art and women have babies?' People used to say that sort of thing. She loved it that I was pregnant though she'd had three abortions. She thought it was romantic. She ran out and bought champagne and we sat on her bed talking all afternoon."

"Where was I born?" I wanted to hear it again.

"In Paris. At the beginning it was gorgeous. I'd wrap you in a sling and walk all over the city. I'd sit inside Notre Dame during the organ practice and then take you over to Shakespeare's to show you off to George who ran the bookstore. I took you to the parks to watch the children pushing their little boats with sticks." Her eyes drifted away contentedly. She loved to tell me about those months of walking. "The light was yellow and it was a quieter city than it is now. After a few months you were a good sleeper. I was sitting with you in a café one morning and I thought, 'I'd like to paint this.' But I had nowhere to work. Your father worked in our studio and I got restless. I took you to the Bois de Boulogne and sometimes I took the train to the Loire. One day sitting by the river I thought, 'North is Normandy and north beyond is England.' That day I knew I'd come home. I missed being able to find a forest, to think of the north. I wanted to work. I loved your father and I took you out each day so he could work but when I was ready to start painting again he simply said, *'Il faut que tu te débrouilles.'* He wouldn't help with you and we couldn't afford a babysitter and the studio was too small to share. I did find a way to paint . . ."

Her voice drifted off into a shade of doubt. Then she looked back at me and suddenly laughed. "I was ready to come back. Besides, there weren't even any squirrels in Paris. Can you imagine what kind of wildlife painter I'd have been over there? Pigeons!"

I could see her, nineteen years old, sitting with me in her arms beside the Loire, trying to work out her life. She always made sure I had three corn-sized kernels of love at the centre. That she loved me. That she'd loved my father. That I must love myself. These three bits she planted and tilled and nurtured in me though they were seeds that didn't always grow easily together.

The pain pierced her from inside out. She tried to keep it hidden under orneriness. She was often thirsty but needed help to get her glass. Pain stripped each physical act to its core. There are things we do alone: give birth, choose when to stay and when to go, choose when to give of ourselves, die. Some we can escape, some not. I'd never been able to fill up all the holes in my mother's life and I couldn't in her dying, either. She was having to do most of it alone. Some days I bundled her up in the car and drove her to the escarpment to see the woods or down to the docks and the lake. There was time and we found love there. But dying slowly is hard work.

One easier morning, I took her to the barns to meet the elephants. Saba came over first and my mother fed her an orange. Kezia ran her trunk fingers up and down her arm. My mother stood in the stillness of the elephants scenting her. She enjoyed it quietly, breathing in the elephant air.

"Look," I said, and I took a penny out of my pocket and flipped it to Saba. She didn't catch it but picked it up dextrously from the floor and gave it back.

"Saba, hand it back to me," I said, flipping it out. This time she snagged it in the air, stopped, unrolled her trunk and handed it deliberately to my mother, who reached out and took it with suprise.

I laughed. Saba had just cracked a joke and she shook her head and flapped her ears in amusement.

"She's telling me she understands the routine and can do it with a twist," I said to my mother. "They love to solve problems, not just follow the drill."

My mother handed me the coin and said, "But what if you really meant she had to pass it to you?"

Saba swayed with pleasure.

"That's where the real intelligence comes in, knowing when it's all right to play around and when she has to be serious. My guess is that they tolerate all this domestic routine only as much as they have to. You've got to give them lots of room for creativity."

"I never thought I'd admire my daughter tossing pennies to a baby elephant . . . they are wonderful aren't they?"

She took another orange out of her pocket, peeled it and placed it, a segment at a time, on her shoulder. Kezia patiently plucked away the tiny pieces and put them in her mouth. The last piece my mother held between her teeth the way she did sometimes with her budgies. Again Kezia, hardly brushing her lips, reached out and took the orange.

"You're a dear old thing aren't you," said my mother in the same voice she used to talk to Moore, stroking Kezia's trunk which had returned looking for another piece.

We wandered out of the barn and stood leaning on the fences looking over the fields toward her house. The day was clear and very cold.

She said, "I can see why you come every day. Your elephants are . . ." and then she started to cough. Her air hunger was the worst part of that awful dying. Every cell in her body craved oxygen and she could not get enough of it for them. She stopped, waited, absorbed her breathlessness and dissolved it somewhere deep inside. I hated it when she accepted, when she took heartbreaking pleasure in doing the simplest tasks, holding her sketch pad, taking a brief walk to smell the late-winter earth. She became childlike then, leaning on me, concentrating on the difficult details of living: breathing, keeping her balance, looking out at the world. We did not hurry. We got into the car and went home. I put on some music and crawled up on her big bed to talk. I brought out the photos again, hoping to please her, but she threw them to the floor. "Put them away, I'm not going to spend my last moment thinking about the past like some idiot old woman! Bring me my sketch pad! Turn on the light. Moore, damn it! Get out of my water!"

I left the house with relief that afternoon when Lottie arrived, and after mucking out the barn I stood leaning against Kezia. The elephant rumbled her greeting to me and when I cried, she dabbed her trunk on my tears and tasted them. She shuffled in close to me and I watched the light skin on her forehead fluttering. I cried and listened to silence inside and out and Kezia made me understand that she would drink as many tears as I had.

<hr>

Jo used me to practise Lear's new trunk-lift for the circus. He was working with the gestures elephants use to move teak trees, grasping the trunk, turning it on its side, balancing it and lifting it in the air. Jo had worked Lear in the sequence using a six-foot log. Now it was time to try it with an acrobat. Jo said to me, "Pretend you're a tree, make your body stiff as you can."

I trusted Lear but I didn't understand at first how to keep my body rigid as a tree. He wrapped his trunk around my torso and lifted but I flopped down, instinctively protecting my belly. With his powerful trunk and neck Lear was able to get me up as if I were a burlap sack and Jo smiled and called, "You're making it hard for him! You've got to keep your arms straight at your sides, hold your legs straight, and keep your head in line with your body." He touched Lear's shoulder and instructed, "Lear, good, down."

Gently Lear placed me on the ground and we tried again. This time I turned my back to the ground and let Lear lift me to the sky. I held my back and legs rigid, his thick, strong trunk wrapped around my waist, and the muscles all through my torso and stomach stretched as I trusted and watched the winter clouds above.

Jo said to Lear, "Up."

Lear rose then on his two back legs, lifting us above the tops of the trees through the frozen air. I thrust my arms out like a performer and in my own weightlessness felt a bubble move in my stomach. Astonished I hung in the air, waiting for my baby to move again. I felt that first wriggle inside me as if I'd seen gold in dross. Jo clapped and tapped Lear's front shoulder to come down. We landed with a little bump as Lear placed his front feet back on the ground, then smoothly he lowered his trunk, and tipped me up to stand. I hugged him and Jo came forward with an orange and a nod of satisfaction. "He's good!"

As my baby grew, I lived constantly in a double kind of awareness. I could muck out and talk to the elephants and the baby at the same time; I could sleep and be aware of the growing inside me at the same time; I could fly through the air and feel her at the same time. And so, as I grew accustomed to living inside and outside at once, I kept my preoccupations to myself and let Jo keep his.

Jo was trying to add what looked like a headstand into the act, a forelegs balance, the trunk folded out and coiled in front of the elephant on the ground. Each time they got to that part, Lear balked and Jo pushed him to work at it. I watched from the fence and it was terrible to see how the trunk got in his way, to see Jo prodding his hind hips to push them up. Lear could not get his balance. They'd been working on it for weeks. When Lear stood again his head drooped in frustration.

"Why don't you just drop that move?" I asked.

"I know he can do it."

"But it doesn't look very natural."

"People walking on their hands isn't very natural either, but they still do it."

I loved Jo, with his long blond hair falling out from behind his ears and his gentle hands on the animals and on me. I loved his expertise with the elephants. I loved the smell of a winter afternoon out in the field and talking to him. I didn't like to see Lear feel dread and failure. I didn't like the way Jo's face set hard with Lear.

"Maybe you're pushing Lear too hard. He does the rest of the routine so well."

"How do you think elephants dig their wells during a drought? They thrust their trunks down and balance forward when they have to. The move is completely natural."

"Except there's no thirst."

I knew better than to argue with Jo about his elephants, but he'd said they get unruly at Lear's age. "Jo, do you ever worry about Lear getting older? What do they do with Africans when they won't behave any more?"

"They chain them up and keep them separate. They make them into living statues. They don't touch them any more and they put them behind hydraulic doors. Why do you think I'm working him so much? The longer I keep him attentive to me, the longer he can stay alive."

⸻ ◆ ⸻

Circus season got Jo off the Safari and out of the usual routine. The tiny worry lines between his brows flattened. He bathed and groomed the elephants, cleaned the trailers and tack. He unfolded Gertrude's gold-embroidered headpiece that tapered to the end of her trunk and tied off with a red silk tassel. Then he spread out her padded silk cape, which draped to the ground from her shoulders to her rump and was covered with thousands of hand-sewn gold sequins. When Gertrude was dressed up she walked soberly around the yard. Together we checked the enormous headpiece and blanket for tears, loose threads and lost sequins. In India this kind of elephant costume was used for carrying relics in religious parades.

I was surprised at how much I missed Jo when he was away. He drove back when he got a day off, even if he was too far to bring the elephants. The first time he drove all night and arrived back at six in the morning. I was waiting in the barn when I heard his truck pull up. I was in his arms and breathing in the smell of him before he was through the door.

"Don't go back," I said, "send a courier for Lear and Gertrude."

We walked around the barn together, greeting the elephants, exchanging bits of stories, and when we'd exclaimed together over Saba and Alice and Kezia, Jo pulled me away from them to an alcove with a roof of inwoven shade against the east wall. I sat astride him and I could feel his familiar thighs through my jeans and I knew I'd be happiest to seek no happier state. He slipped his left hand under my shirt and caressed my swollen breasts. He breathed on my lips and I was straining toward him when he said, "Are you pregnant?"

"Yes."

"Us?"

I had to smile. I hadn't been anywhere but the barn and at my mother's since I'd met Jo.

"Yes," and then trying to tease him I surprised myself, "Now, you won't go off and leave me any more."

Jo took his hand from my breast and wrapped me in so close that I could feel his heart. With the same dry voice I noticed the first time we met, he observed, "Seems like you're the one more likely to leave. I'll be here, but elephants are migratory animals. They like to move around."

ALECTO

During the lengthening days of that early spring, though cold winds still pierced my skin, the smell of the warming earth was so strong I felt like eating it. Alecto appeared at the barn one afternoon, excited. He reached inside his jacket and pulled out an article he had just published entitled, "Notes on the heart, liver and lung of a female elephant (Indian)" in a journal called *Loxodonta* published by the State University of Florida. I flipped through it and saw the usual academic histology: dissections, descriptions, disease possibilities based on colour, texture and size.

"What do you think of it?" he wrote on his board.

"It seems interesting."

He pointed to the author credit under the title and scribbled on his board, "I wrote it."

"I can see that. Alecto, why are you hanging around here?"

He began to write, erased what he'd written and started again. "When I heard Lear might die, I came to do an autopsy."

"But he's better now."

He looked hurt, wrote on his board and handed it to me with a mocking smile, "I wanted to get to know you better."

I climbed up the ladder, threw some fresh bales down, spread them around and filled the water trough. Then I sat and quickly read his paper. He had taken measurements of the thickness of the organ walls, the veins, the arteries, the connective tissues. By the end of his paper I knew about the diseased organs of a single female elephant kept in a tiny zoo for thirteen years.

We walked together out to the yard and watched the early spring light, the thawing trees, the softening fields. The strangeness of the elephant barns and talking to Alecto was hearing only my own voice. All my conversations were so silent. I handed his paper back.

"What would have helped her?"

"More exercise," he wrote.

"Why not draw a conclusion like that in your paper?"

"Not provable. Besides, it makes the zoo look bad."

"Then why do the work?"

He frowned impatiently and quickly made a list down three columns of his board, connecting things with lines and arrows: "Birth weight, growth rate, teeth, tusks, food intake, water intake, air displacement, normal body temperature, stool and urine composition, heart, lungs, bones, joints."

I took the board from his hand before he was finished. "But, why really?"

He looked at me with a dismissive smile and wrote, "Aspiring pride and insolence . . . Don't you just want to know?"

"Sometimes."

Then he swept his arm across the fields in front of us, blue in that early spring twilight, and wrote, "I wish I'd made all this, don't you?"

There are people whom nothing shocks. My mother used to say if you read Proust nothing will ever shock you. When I got back to the house my mother had Moore sitting on her lip picking at her teeth and she was flipping through the channels on her television set like some demented crone.

She saw me and said, "Sophie! Back so soon? Off you go, Moore," and she cast the bird from his perch on her lip into the air.

"I was busy today."

"With your elephant man."

"He's still away, that's why it's busy. He's coming back again tomorrow."

"I haven't eaten a thing."

"I'll get something."

"I'm not hungry any more. Alecto's back. He dropped by with lunch. He didn't stay long though. No one does."

I didn't want the guilt or the slow dying tonight. I didn't want pain or waiting. Just for one night.

"Mom, I want a drink. I don't suppose you'd have a little scotch with me?"

She hesitated a moment and said, "I would like that, yes."

Scotch on ice was always our drink. When I came home from school, and later, from Africa on my holidays, we sat and sipped a scotch as soon as I'd thrown down my bags and taken off my shoes. It started in a tiny fishing village in Labrador. The village had five churches and was dry. We'd gone there sketching when I was a teenager. We travelled up the coast on the medical field ship and when the doctors went back to their berths on the boat in the evenings, we slept in the clinic. Each night, my mother dug down in her bag, pulled out a bottle of scotch and said, "Have a nip, it's so much more fun when you're not supposed to."

I went to the kitchen cupboard and took down two crystal scotch tumblers. I clanked a couple of ice cubes into the glasses and poured out the warm liquid. By the time I got back, she was sitting up, patchy hair smoothed, the TV off.

"Alecto brought a new article he published to show me this afternoon. He was all excited."

I handed her drink across the bed. "I know, he brought it to the barn, too. Did you read it?"

"No, I can't read those things. What was it about?"

"It was a heart study."

"He's an entertaining fellow, just cynical enough. Strange today, it exhausted me, as if there's not enough time for his showmanship. There's nothing to him, is there. An empty shell. Full of words he can't even speak any more."

"That's a bit strong."

"Well, he asked today if I had any extra morphine."

"Was he joking?"

"He tried to turn it into a joke. But if I'd offered, he would have taken it."

"I have a feeling he's become a regular down the road, too. . . . I told him you get tired easily. Just kick him out when he stays too long. Jo wishes he'd leave but he won't say anything. He says Alecto's like a tick that gets buried under your skin."

I drank quickly, letting the golden liquid roll around the back of my throat. I looked at her yellow skin. Her eyes were bright, her breathing heavy.

"I wouldn't get involved with him if I were you . . . if you're tempted, I mean. Men like that are trouble . . . they never stay if their own pleasure's at stake."

"For heaven's sake . . ."

"I mean even on work things. He's ambitious."

I poured myself another drink and held out the bottle to her. She nodded cheerfully and when I poured she held down my hand until her tumbler was half full. I raised my eyebrows and she said, "To hell with it, Sophie. I used to love our drinks together. What's the difference?"

I heard her loneliness rattling around like a pea in a dried-up pod. It was good to drink with her again. I felt the liquid roll smooth down my throat and spread warmly through me. "If you could do anything you wanted to right now, what would you do?"

"I'd not be dying."

"I know, but what else."

She nibbled at the rim of her glass, then sat back stiffly as people who spend a lot of time in bed do. Finally she said, "I'd put on a wig and lots of make-up and a wild dress. I'd find out where there was an opening, someone else's, look at some art, then go to a restaurant with dancing."

I could see her as the young mother I'd lived alone with, in the daytime little flecks of paint on her hands, her eyes gazing far away, her lovely big-lipped smile as she showed me a twig or a moth's wing under a magnifying glass, and in the evenings sitting across the kitchen table doing her nails while I watched, both of us smelling of bubble bath because I always went in with her, the fancy nail kit open between us, cuticle-pusher and tiny scissors and mother-of-pearl-handled files. "I have awful nails, Sophie," she'd say, holding them up boldly. It was true. They were stained from her paints and broken and never all the same length. But she carefully painted each with three quick strokes of red and waved them in the air singing, "Teddy Bear, Teddy Bear, turn out the light, Teddy Bear, Teddy Bear, say goodnight." By then the babysitter would have arrived and she was off, and I wondered under the covers where adults go and what adults do at night.

I shifted to the edge of the bed and said, "Let's do it now, let's get dressed, put on make-up, call a taxi, go out."

I wanted her dying to be suddenly a mistake, to escape just one last time.

"Soph, I can't."

"Sure you can, just once, come on, I'll do your nails."

I was already off her bed and in the bathroom gathering up bottles, cotton, a towel, make-up. I laid them all out on the sheets, took her hands and started. When I touched her I felt her body sucking my warmth. I massaged her often, trying to rub life into her, and she'd melt against me and say, "Oh that does feel good."

But that night I sipped my scotch and vigorously filed her nails, then began to push back her cuticles, and she yelped, "Ouch, that hurts, Soph, slow down."

I shook the nail polish bottle and spread her hands out on the towel. I tried to do it the way she always did, three swift overlapping strokes, but my strokes faltered and I had to wipe at the edges. She hung her hands in the air and smiling now said, "Soph, hand my drink to me, I don't want to smudge," and I held her glass to her lips not because she was weak but because her nail polish was drying.

Then I started in on my own ragged nails, dirty and chipped and broken from the barn work. She was shaking the nail polish she'd chosen for me, a deep red called *Burnt Sierra,* and she brushed it on expertly, her face clear and happy.

In the early days of her illness she'd bought two human-hair wigs. One was auburn, shoulder-length with bangs, and the other a short curly dark-haired one, a kind of pixie cut. She said, "If I have to be bald, I'm going to have fun with it."

They sat on styrofoam heads on her dresser. The budgies

sometimes landed on them, pulling and stealing strands of hair, and if she wasn't looking I'd throw things at the birds. I went over to the dresser, plucked away the more glamorous red one and plonked it on my head. I was transformed. My mother enjoyed that wig. It changed her so much that people didn't recognize her.

"Remember when you wore this wig to the Rendez-Vous?" I asked. "You said you got too hot and pulled it off and stuck it in your purse."

"Yes," she laughed. "That was such a humid night. Throw me the short one. It was a wonderful evening. I was still quite well. I thought the maitre d' was going to put me out ..."

I started my own make-up, building my skin tone, cheeks, eyes—lashes and lids—all from the hue of the wig. Then I found a good lipstick that picked up my nails. My mother looked wonderful with hair on. She put colour on her face in wide, bold strokes, a lovely ruddiness in her cheeks, a promising sensuality to her large lips. She had always liked to take time with her lips and used a tiny brush to outline them before she filled in the fleshy part with a darker colour. She enlarged her eyes with great thick lashes, drew on a hint of eyebrows to peep out from under her bangs and lightly covered up the dark smudges below her eyes. She put on a pair of earrings I'd sent her from Africa and slipped some of my malachite bracelets around her wrists. Finally, I held up a tiny hand-mirror for her to see. "You're beautiful."

"Not bad," she said, laughing and flipping the mirror to

face me. "Come here, let me give you a little more blush. There ... lovely."

I looked at her and said, "Lovely."

"I meant you."

"I know, and I meant you."

She pulled my chin in lightly, told me to look up and brought the blue-black mascara brush up under my lashes.

"Now which dress?" I asked.

She played along and said she'd wear her green silk, the one she'd worn to the Rendez-Vous. I went to the closet and dug around. In the middle were her dressing gowns and two loose track suits so popular with those who tend the elderly and the dying. One of the afternoon nurses had brought them but she wouldn't put them on. I dug deeper, looking through the clothes she hadn't worn in months, found her green dress and pushed hangers back until I saw her black taffeta cocktail dress, fitted, no shoulders, a nipped-in waist, one I remembered from years ago.

"Can I wear this?"

"Where did you find that?" she said, laughing. "It may not go round your waist, we were awful about our waists for those dresses. Try it on."

I wriggled in from the bottom, and the waist wouldn't close but the rest of it was fine. I left the side zipper open. The old material was crisp against my skin. Moore dove down to try to land on one of my bare shoulders and I flicked him off my neck in one of his theatrical panicked flutters.

My mother looked almost happy sitting up in bed, wearing her wig, some colour in her cheeks, our make-up and towels and tissues in a jumble in front of her. Through my scotch haze, I was determined now and said, "I'm calling the cab."

I threw her dress on the bed, pulled back the bedcovers to swing out her legs and slip it on. Angry, she pulled back. "Sophie, stop, I can't, I really can't!"

Tears fell from her eyes and all that beauty melted away. Her bright fingers wiped at her tears and she tore off her wig. Shocked and angry with my own drunkenness, now I was crying too, and when I wiped my eyes mascara streaked over my fists and the thick lipstick tasted of salt.

"I'm sorry."

"Hand me the cold cream, will you?" she said, her tears great round drops from her diamond will, and I loathed myself and I smeared away my make-up and when she was done with hers, in seven or eight great sweeping slashes of her hands, she reached over and took off bits I'd missed.

"Don't cry, Sophie ... it doesn't matter ... don't you hate the feeling of cold cream, I'm going to wash it off, I don't care if my skin does shrivel up," she said, swinging out of bed stiffly. She tossed the bottles and brushes and clothes into a basket and carried it all slowly into the bathroom. I followed her and stood near her as she ran the water to warm. Side by side we scrubbed our faces. We wiped at the smudges and removed the colour. We dabbed astringent on cotton balls and took off every bit right down into our pores. Then we splashed cool water on our skin. As we were patting ourselves dry with fresh towels, my mother pulled my face in close to hers and made me look in the big mirror, cheek to cheek with her. The mirror's sides reflected back a tunnel of faces, each the same, narrowing down and down. Her face was tired, her head nearly bald, her skin the colour of yellowing wax with no eyebrows, deep rings under her eyes and deep pain furrows above her nose. My own eyes were red and swollen, my short, thick hair was tousled over thick eyebrows, and though I was tired, my skin shone with my baby and my long healthy afternoons at the Safari. I could feel the clean coldness of her delicate cheek on my own warm one as we stared at ourselves in the mirror, scrubbed and plain, and she kept her hand there, pressing me to her until we blurred and became one image.

———❖———

I was upstairs in the loft when I heard Lear bellow, a sound I'd never heard before. I scrambled down the ladder and was through the barn and out to the field in moments. Lear's head was low, his ears held wide, and he was running. Jo was running for the fence and Lear's trunk was extended. Lear thwacked Jo's back with the tip of his trunk. Jo fell and before he hit the ground Lear hit him again, this time throwing him sideways into the soft earth. I screamed and ran to the fence yelling, "Lear!"

The elephant ran forward and tried to stamp on Jo, who

was tumbling across the dirt toward the fence like a bit of old wool. Jo froze and just as Lear was above him he rolled under the elephant. Instinctively courageous, he grabbed onto his left front leg, clinging like a bloodsucker, his cheek and forearms scraping up and down against the elephant's rough hide. Lear thrashed his leg wildly, dropped his trunk, curled it firmly around Jo's right leg, snapped Jo off and flung him through the air. Then Lear charged again. A flat crack echoed across the field and Lear's head jerked back and to the side in an odd twisting movement. He crumpled forward on his trunk into the ground, only a few steps from Jo. The noise was gunshot and blood trickled from Lear's forehead where a single, precise shot through the brain had felled him. He looked now like a pretend elephant splayed on the ground. The field was torn up, deep gulleys and drag marks through the blood-soaked earth around Jo's face and arms. He was moaning lightly. A sandpiper on its spring migration whistled sharply somewhere in the trees. I jumped over the fence and was leaning over Jo before Alecto could join us, his gun dropped casually back in his pocket.

This was how I lost Jo.

ELEPHANT-ENGLISH
DICTIONARY
PART THREE

The Functionals

There are a number of activities in elephant life that are concerned with survival: migration, the search for food and water, the safety of the group. Even at the Safari, where physical safety is more or less ensured, the elephants use functional language constantly, indicating to me that the need to share food, water and safety is essential to their moral survival.

When the Safari elephants are separated, they keep track of each other by rumbling locating songs and contact songs. They use their Let's go rumble whenever they move off in unison, even over a short distance. They let each other know about food, water and imminent threats. Finally, they acknowledge what I call wonder or the sacred in their quotidian rumbling. I include this as one of the functionals because these utterances are as frequent as references to food and water and I suspect that without them their survival as a group would be meaningless.

*mro ahah: (14-18 Hz.) Contact call.

When the elephants are separated, they sing this song in an overlapping spondaic chant with a contact response *(see *mro ohoh).*

I first discovered contact calls when I was recording in the barn and Gertrude moved deliberately to the east wall and stood facing it, rumbling. I went outside and discovered Alice at precisely the same place on the other side of the wall singing her response song. If the wall had been removed the two elephants would have been standing face to face. In the wild it is thought that contact songs keep groups intact over distances of several kilometres.

*mro ohoh: (14-18 Hz.) Contact response. An answer to the contact call.

*mrah: (18-25 Hz.) Interrogative locating rumble.

While an elephant is foraging or figuring out a problem or working or dreaming, she might forget to keep track of the rest of the group. When she suddenly discovers this, she'll utter a locating rumble, stop and listen for a response.

*mroo: (18-25 Hz.) Response locating rumble. A successful answer locates the separated elephant and commonly resolves into a contact response song *(see *mro ohoh).*

All locating and contact rumbles are derived from the four utterances above. Each elephant sings her calls and responses, varying the timbre, rhythm and ornamentation to make the songs personal. I listen eagerly to our young elephants creating their personal locating and response songs.

grah~: (20 Hz.) Let's go rumble.

This is one of Elephant's most frequent utterances, usually by the matriarch, and in her absence, the leader of the group. When they hear it the elephants freeze, lift their ears to listen, then turn simultaneously and begin to move away. The first time I saw this I had the same feeling I had when I read e. e. cummings' lines

— listen: there's a hell
of a good universe next door; let's go

^ar: (55+ Hz.) Warning.

Short, sharp snort, accompanied by the ears spreading and a firm move forward. It is a signal to beware, before anger or aggression. I've heard this used occasionally against an interfering raccoon or a pesky red-winged blackbird and once when a lion escaped into the elephant area. If a human hears this, they should freeze, move slowly backwards and get out of the elephant's way as precipitously as possible.

gr^or: (18 Hz.) Danger.

Short, infrasonic snort, accompanied by the ears spreading and intense listening. It is a signal to other elephants to stop and beware, that there may be danger in the immediate environment. It is often followed by a Let's go rumble *(see grah)*.

poor^rrr: (20-22 Hz.) Food.

The discovery of food is marked by this utterance in anapestic rhythm which resolves into a spondaic during grazing, and is accompanied by a pleasure utterance *(see rii)*.

pra pra: (50 Hz.) Tiny growl by a hungry calf, meaning simply, "I'm hungry."

This is one of the first sounds a young elephant makes, asking for the mother (who is rarely more than a few feet away) to nurse. I have heard Gertrude join our babies singing *pra pra* to a reluctant mother, urging them to get on with things.

*owrr~rr: (23 Hz.) Water.

This is a good example of rhythm affecting a word's meaning. It is uttered using an insistent iambic when the elephant is thirsty, and as a rolling spondaic in combination with a pleasure utterance *(see rii)* when bathing and playing in the water.

mwo~oo~mwo: (22 Hz.) Archaic, rare. A female migration contact song.

Elephants are migratory, but we have no provision for migratory behaviour in captivity. In the wild, migration songs may be used to keep in contact with members of a group as it moves over great distances.

I was once commissioned to bring Kezia and Gertrude on a ten-day walk protesting women's poverty. Each day I walked with the elephants in the company of three thousand women toward Parliament Hill. Kezia and Gertrude were sometimes separated, one near the beginning, one near the end of the march, and they rumbled this song hypnotically throughout the day. The song, so effortless and rhythmic, was well suited to a long trek.

broo: (14 Hz.) A male migration song.

Our sole male, Lear, was the only elephant to sing this unusually beautiful song while he roamed alone. I think of it as a "road song" for solitary wandering in search of food. It reminds me of a line from the Buddhist Basket of Discourses, "Better to live alone; with a fool there is no companionship. With few desires, live alone and do no evil, like an elephant in the forest roaming at will."

Among the great tragedies of Lear's death is that young males lose another chance to learn their wandering songs.

*waohm: (12 Hz.) Expression of wonder or the sacred, highly varied rhythms according to context.

This was a difficult utterance to isolate because it is buried in so many other songs. I first identified it when I was hired by a group of Buddhists living in Hamilton to enact a candlelight procession for their Festival of Light. We dressed Kezia in her gold-threaded headpiece and cape, and she carried a relic of the Buddha on her back in a candlelit procession. All through the parade she sang this syllable in a lovely modulating spondaic rhythm with little ornament or variation. I can only guess that this is her sacred song, remembered from infancy in India, when she would have been surrounded by other elephants on the Ganges during sacred ceremonies. After the procession, I began to hear it all through the Elephant songs and I realized that it is woven into many daily activities as subtly as breath.

A SLICE *of* ELEPHANT

What do you do with a dead elephant?

When I was in Africa, I went out with a ranger in a Land-Rover to look at the bones of an elephant killed by poachers two days earlier. Lions and vultures had already stripped the skeleton clean and as we approached we saw a small group of elephants gathered there. We stopped upwind and watched them circle the bones, scuff at, push and scatter them, then spread dust over them with their trunks. After several hours the group moved off leaving a small elephant, about four or five years old, behind. The driver, no longer afraid, reached to his keys to turn on his engine, but I begged him to stay a little longer. And so we sat and watched. The small elephant mimicked her elders, smelling the bones, pushing them, trying to spread dust over them. The driver said softly, "Go back little one, there are lions."

It is eerie to see a small animal alone in the open in Africa. There are so many threats. I kept checking the bushes and the trees for hyenas and lions. I asked the ranger why

the usually protective herd would let this little one stay alone, and he said, "They have to eat and drink. They don't have any choice."

"Why?"

"That little one won't go. She did this yesterday, too. They came back for her at night. Perhaps tonight she'll give it up."

"But why does she keep staying?"

"The bones are her mother's."

"I wonder if I'll want to stay with my mother's bones when she's dead," I said.

The ranger, a young man who had spent his life in the bush silently watching, answered drily, "I wonder, would you risk your life to do it."

———◆———

Jo's body survived the accident with Lear. He'd been courageous during the battle and he had lived. His jaw was broken, his face a mass of bruises. His shoulder was dislocated and he had a concussion. His spleen was ruptured but he was stable.

When I came into his room Alecto was there, sitting in the corner and Jo lay, his hair shaved, head wrapped, shoulder strapped, an IV in one arm and oxygen in his nostrils. He was conscious but his jaw was wired closed. I went to the side of his bed and gently lifted his hand. He opened his eyes and he could not smile or reach for me. His brother had already been contacted and he'd asked that they transfer him to a hospital in Florida. I told the doctors that we could take care of him but they only said, "Are you next of kin?" and then, "He has indicated he will go."

I was afraid to stroke his face and afraid to touch his head and hands. All of him was battered. I took some hair they had not shaved and I held it lightly, wrapping it around my finger. I thought I saw the tightening at the corner of his mouth that came before his familiar smile, and his eyes softened.

"Jo."

There was nothing but his name.

We sat together quietly as nurses came in and out checking monitors and IVs. Jo dozed off. Alecto had brought some food from the cafeteria and he offered me a coffee and a piece of sandwich.

"Thank God you were there."

He nodded. His board was on the floor.

We sat until Jo stirred and this time I held his hands, touched his face. In the late evening we watched other visitors leaving down the echoing hallways and the ward quietened and darkened. A nurse came in to check his blood pressure and said, "The visiting time is over. We'll be settling everyone for the night now."

"Won't you be waking him once an hour for his concussion?"

"Yes, that's the routine."

"Well then it doesn't much matter if I'm here, does it?"

I was impatient with hospital rules those days. "Jo, can you hear me?"

He opened his eyes and clearly saw me, recognized me.

"You've had a concussion. Did they tell you? They're going to keep waking you up tonight. Too bad it's not me. We'd have more fun."

He moved his finger on my palm.

"I'll check the elephants when I go back. I phoned the circus to cancel for you. They were fine about it."

I avoided talking about Lear. I hadn't really thought about that great body lying there.

Jo blinked wearily.

"They want me to go now, I'll come again first thing in the morning. Jo, you don't have to go away. We can manage here."

But he'd closed his eyes.

Alecto stepped up to the bed. He held out his board to me, and to Jo. "I have to go. I'm doing an autopsy overnight. The rendering truck comes in the morning."

Jo half opened his eyes, read it slowly and looked at me for help.

Alecto wrote on his board and handed it to me. "The Safari gave permission in Jo's absence."

"Jo doesn't want you to do one. Who's going to control the other elephants? We can't risk any more problems."

Alecto shrugged and headed for the door.

I followed him out into the hall and pulled at his sleeve. He turned to face me, his body tight with pleasure, and wrote, "You should come, you're really going to see something."

"You know Jo doesn't want you to do this. It upsets the other animals. It's pointless. We already know the cause of death. Why would you?"

He wrote quickly on his board, "Why do you keep asking why? It is settled."

Then he left.

———◆———

When pain is extreme for people ill like my mother, one of the last things they can do is block nerves so nothing at all is felt. They blocked my mother's brachial plexus, cutting off feeling through her right arm and hand. She could still move them but she could no longer feel them. She had to be protected from burning, bruising and cutting herself. She joked that she wanted all her morphine injections in her right side. It didn't feel safe any more to leave her in the house by herself.

"The worst part of dying is you never get to be alone," she complained.

But when I left the room she'd call out for me.

I got back late the night Jo was attacked. I came in through the door quietly and tried to settle myself before I walked into the bedroom. I had telephoned from the hospital to ask Lottie to stay late. She was dozing on a big chair beside my mother's bed and didn't waken when I came in. The two Grays were perched cosily on the arm of her chair. Lottie was the only person besides my mother they weren't skittish with. I touched Lottie's arm and she woke up quickly.

"I'm sorry Lottie, I hate waking people up."

"That's all right dearie, nurses don't sleep that soundly," and she stretched and smiled under her flattened crown of wiry grey hair.

"Did she take her morphine this evening?"

"Yes. She was on oxygen most of the day. She had a lot of pain this evening."

I wondered if my mother was taking her morphine or hiding it. I knew she'd been lying about how many break-through injections she gave herself. She had four extra vials in a locked box in the bathroom closet.

"Can you come tomorrow, mid-morning? They're going to need me over at the Safari to get things organized, with Jo off."

Lottie shook her head empathetically and said, "You've got a lot on your plate now, dearie."

The outside world seemed so distant once Lottie was gone and I stood over my mother's bed. I stared down at her sleeping and she opened her eyes and seemed awake, the difference between waking and sleeping growing less and less. I think people who are sick for a long time grow used to being asleep. They rouse and if the pain is not too much they drift back into a dream or a conversation wherever they left it.

"Lottie, did you see Moore trying to lift me away?"

"Mom, it's me."

"Sophie, you're back . . ." I felt her waking now.

"How are you?"

"Lottie said your elephant man got hurt."

"Yes. Did anyone manage to open a window in here today?"

We had fallen into these gentle predictable jokes, teasing words meant to soothe and fill in the silence. We spoke less than we ever had in our lives, but the most mundane of our exchanges were charged with compassion.

"What happened?"

I sat on the edge of the bed. I told her briefly about the attack.

"Jo's in the hospital. He's going to make it but he got a concussion."

"What happened to the elephant?"

"They shot him."

"Oh."

"They're doing an autopsy tonight."

"My God."

She lay looking at me and then she said, "I wonder why he attacked?"

"Jo's been pushing him hard . . . I don't know."

My mother smiled lightly. "It is hard to imagine pushing an elephant."

"Africans get unpredictable at his age, that's what Jo said. But how do you retire an elephant?" I could see Lear falling onto the field, Jo lying in blood.

"Why are they doing an autopsy?"

"I don't know, to find out more about them."

"Did your elephant man order it?"

"No. His jaw's broken."

"It's Alecto, isn't it?"

I nodded and could hear the hum of the clock beside her bed.

"Did you try to stop it?"

"I couldn't. He went over my head."

"You should try."

"It's futile."

From the still throne of her bed, my mother's face was translucent and drawn.

"You want to go see, don't you?"

I hadn't admitted it to myself. "Yes. I'm curious."

"Sophie, I wouldn't go."

"Why?"

Her grey eyes were grave and piercing. All my life I had the feeling that she saw beyond me.

"You've always thought Jo has a sixth sense about these things."

"He thought he knew Lear, too."

"Why would you want to see such a thing?"

"I don't know. I may never have the chance again."

"Alecto will be in his element. Stay out of his way. What do you think your elephant man will say?"

When I was growing up, we often looked together at anatomy books about the small birds and animals she was painting. She had a skeleton of an owl that she kept on the kitchen counter for weeks. We examined the bones together and she showed me how the joints worked. We looked at how its magnificent head could turn around and where the wide, powerful wings joined the body. She told me the tales of Michelangelo secretly dissecting human bodies to see inside how they worked. But tonight she advised me not to look at the animal I'd grown to know most intimately. I could not understand. After she'd eaten a bit of soft egg and drunk a few sips of water, she drifted off to sleep again. She usually relaxed when I was home, a thought that exhausted me even more. I settled myself into my own bed on the other side of the wall and fell into a light sleep.

I woke at 4:30 because of her awful wheezing. I put her on the oxygen tank and I gave her a shoulder rub and some water to drink and she fell back to sleep. I wandered in the darkness out to the kitchen. The budgies were all still, half asleep on their various perches around the house. Through the back window I could see lights hanging from trees in the paddock, above where Lear's body lay splayed on the ground.

I watched shadows moving below the lights and wondered what was going on there. I told myself I was just going to pay my last respects. It took nothing to decide. She'd sleep another hour and a half. That was all I needed. I was her witness and her comfort but I could not lose myself in her dying. I needed to check the elephants. I listened to her breathing once more then slipped away from her room, through the back door and across the field.

It was a new moon, and as I got closer I could see beams of artificial light through the winter darkness. In the shadows the great skeleton lay wet and gleaming, large flaps of skin rolled back, a row of enormous organs laid neatly out on the ground beside heaps of hacked-off flesh. They'd suspended two floodlights from the trees and had a row of lanterns illuminating the primary organs—liver, lungs, stomach, intestines, spleen, heart—all carefully displayed on a tarp. Alecto was working with three young men from the rendering plant who helped him cut and drag and weigh and stack. They were soaked with blood, their gloves glistening. Each man had a towel hooked in his belt to wipe his hands on so they wouldn't slip on the next cut. All night they'd been hacking and pulling and sorting. Great squares of elephant flesh were stacked knee high, surrounding the work area like a grey igloo. They'd sawed the tusks off the head and unfurled the skin of the trunk to look at its complex muscles. Poor Lear's eyes were open, still staring out.

The air smelled of the stench of things torn limb-meale. The men were soaked to their ankles in spring mud and elephant blood and body fluids. They worked in T-shirts despite the cold, their arms bulging with the night's cutting and hauling.

Alecto was inside Lear, under the great arch of his ribs, carefully measuring each one. His face was serene, his lips lightly together, his breathing easy and concentrated. I watched him in the half-light before he knew I was there, in his face deep scars of thunder, absorbed in lists of numbers. When he saw me his mask of irony slipped back down and he came over and wrote on his pad, "You've missed it, we're done."

He showed me a second clipboard with a slim light taped on the top, where his stacks of paper were clamped down. They'd been working for eight hours and they'd weighed and measured every bit of that elephant. The top sheet was a simple chart:

LEAR

Organ or part	Weight (Kilo)
Liver	42.2
Blood, small part	47.6
Heart	15.6
Lungs (including muscle and other tissue)	157.9
Stomach, intestines, etc. (washed out — empty)	220.4

Hide, whole 69.4

Trunk musculature (estimate from section) . . . 610.1

Muscle (loose) 1651.6

Bones (roughened out), not all 608.5

Front and hind legs (right). 601.4

Right testicle 1.6

Left testicle 1.8

Right kidney 3.6

Left kidney 4.1

Intestinal contents. 337.9

Spleen 18.1

Urine 30.5

Faeces 51.6

Hoof (right front) 19.0

Hoof (right rear) 25.9

Tail. 0.2

Total Weight. . . . .

Under the top sheet was a sheaf of stained paper, short forms and numbers and arrows scratched at odd places, observations that would later appear as autopsy notes.

Loxodonta africanus

Habitat: Florida, southern Ontario
App. 21 years old, adult male
Cause of death: gunshot

Height at shoulder (alive): 3 metres
Weight (alive) app.: 5.5 tonnes
Died: 3 p.m. April 26.

Lung: flaccid, soft; gray and red mottled. Bronchi firm and stand open. Around one in upper lobe of right lung, large area of cheesy degeneration, a zone of connective tissue formed around. This extends above the bronchus in a sheath-like manner. The trachea appears normal. Tubercle bacilli could be demonstrated in the cheesy nodules.

Heart: 15.6 kg. 56 x 32 cm. empty. Left ventricle wall varies in thickness from 6-8 cm. Right ventricle 1.5-2 cm. Muscle firm in consistency and normal in colour. Peri, epi and endocardia pale, smooth, transparent. Valves normal. Mitral is slightly rough on superior surface, smooth and normally resilient. 10 cm. above the valves it measures 2.5 cm. Pulmonary artery measures 2 cm. at the same place. Three areas of thickening, with pale fibrous zone around them in the sinus around the opening of anterior coronary artery, proximal to the semilunar fold of the wall at the origin of the left lateral branch.

Joints: swollen, in right, hind, second joint there is especially large accumulation. Tip end of right femus ulcerated at the edge where cartilage joins the bone.

All the carpal and tarsal joints and the articulations of these with the phalanges, cartilages are irregular and hard. Evidence of long-standing arthritis in every joint. No calcareous deposits.

More pages described the condition of the liver, spleen, kidney, adrenals, but I had no more heart to read it.

The rendering men stood, waiting for Alecto's orders. He checked his watch and wrote, "2 hours until the truck comes. Clean up. Go to the office and wait. I'll come and get you."

They ran hoses over their shovels and pitchforks and crouched around buckets of cold water cleaning their long knives and saws. They piled them neatly on a feed sack and then they turned off the floodlights, swung them down from the trees and rolled up the extension cords they'd run from the barn. As the lights disappeared I stared at the piles of organs until it was too dark to see. We watched the three young men disappear into the darkness of the Safari and when they were gone Alecto turned to me and wrote, "I'm surprised you came."

"I wanted to see."

"You still can."

"Anything unexpected?"

He shook his head proudly. "I've done so many of these. I've seen it all."

I could smell elephant dung on him. His eyes were ringed black with his night's labours and his exhausted face was unshaven blue. He beckoned me to follow him as he walked along the animal's viscera, astonishing in their size, intestines metres long, slices and chunks of many-hued organs spread out on plastic sheets. We stopped before the enormous heart, which had been sliced in quarters and laid back together. Alecto nudged it with his foot and pointed his light at the top left quadrant.

"Should be a fatty mantle here," he wrote. "In the wild there's lots."

"Why isn't it here?"

"Don't know. Probably too little exercise."

He flashed his light along the outside shape of the brain, lifting it from the front to show me the folds of the underside. "See how there are many convolutions in the forebrain," he wrote, "I love this," and he quickly erased it.

"What is it you love?"

"Its brain is heavier and larger than any living or extinct mammal," he wrote and continued, "The cerebellum has an anterior lobe, like us, and lobule I is strongly developed."

He put down his board, knelt and showed me the folds separating the lobes. Then he wrote, "Elephant brains are small at birth and they have to grow, like humans. They're designed to learn. It's not all built in from the beginning."

He pointed to the individual lobules and wrote, "Subdivided lobules. Proportionately, their lobules outnumber those in a human cerebellum."

I read it slowly. "What does that mean?"

"We don't know. It's a characteristic of specialized mammals."

Then he balanced his board again and showed me the hole where the bullet had gone in.

"Did you find the bullet?"

He ignored me and straightened, stretching his stiff knees while I continued to stare. When I finally stood, his eyes caught mine. I felt his lustful reverence for this single heart bigger than a bushel basket of potatoes, for this brain as old as the earth. He contemplated them with a fascination I'd never seen in him in the barns. I looked up and saw his mouth open and close as if he were chewing the air.

Dawn was near, snapping the branches on the trees in the ribbed cold, stirring awake the darkened minds of any Safari animals that still slept. I knew the elephants in the barn had been awake and distressed all night, scenting Lear's blood through the walls, trying to get to him. The shadows were cracked apart by the sound of Alecto breathing, all unsmoothed air and coiled effort.

He looked at his watch, and wrote, "I have one more set of measurements on the skeleton. Can you help?"

We stepped inside the stripped bones. The great ribs arched upwards like praying hands and through them I could see a low winter sky clouded with morning snow clouds. The temperature was dropping, there would be storms that day. I might keep the elephants in, play with them in the barn, try to bury the odours of Lear.

Alecto removed his little penlight and handed it to me

with the end of his tape measure. We inched along side by side from the wide area at the collarbone behind the animal's great neck and head. There was a terrible smell from the flesh and the great ears hung down backwards over the bones above us. I wondered whether he'd noted the structure of the eardrum or if he'd looked for the place in the forehead where they make their rumbles. I could see from the inside how the enormous arteries and veins that fed the head intersected across the skull. Alecto had scraped off enough of the flesh to measure the back of the skull's circumference. I could look straight into the jaw. I peered up to the thin flesh that I thought must be the source of elephant paunsing.

"Hold the tape and move along toward the tail," wrote Alecto, and he began to release the tape along the vertebrae. As I crouched back he placed and held down his end. He took a small ruler out of his breast pocket and carefully measured the depth of each vertebra, making little sketches as he went along. From standing almost upright, I bent, then crawled into the hips and tail area where the ribs narrowed. I stretched my arm out and held the tape at what I thought was the end of the tailbone. Alecto worked fastidiously, remeasuring the size of the small vertebra at the tail twice, then checked my tape placement. Now I could hear the lioness's dawn calls, captive birds woken by wild ones, the hyenas agitated by the smell of so much blood, the elephants shuffling inside, trying to get to poor Lear.

I was overcome with pity, and before Alecto had finished

his reading I pressed the button and snapped closed the measure. I could feel his warmth beside me. We were touching hip to hip, shoulder to shoulder inside the skeleton and his body heat burned away what was left between us. He looked at me sharply, and when he saw I had pulled the tape away from him intentionally his hand shot out and twisted my jaw, his lips pressed against mine and his obdurate tongue thrust into my mouth. His unusual weight rolled heavily on me, tipping me off balance and backwards, pinning me under him. He tore at my pants and the elastic gave way easily. The ribs of the elephant pressed into my tailbone and cold mud squeezed up, soaking me. His forearm was across my chest holding me down and his other hand was struggling with his own clothes. For a few seconds I was so shocked that I did nothing. I looked through the bony cage of the elephant and lay utterly still. I saw a branch in a tree over us and then I hooked my heels into a rib and pushed myself back, jamming the top of my skull against bones. I swung my arm up and smashed the tape measure against his brow, cutting it, watching the blood spurt out over me. I raised my leg and he forced it down, driving my heel into a rock. I kicked him hard again and managed to set him off balance enough to scramble out from under him. Shining dewdrops hung from the bones and my pregnant stomach was between us, exposed and fleshy white. I got far enough sideways to squeeze through two of the ribs and I fell out into the wet, blood-soaked ground. Across the open field in the grey dawn were the barns, the fences, the paddock. Jo had been walking there with Lear just yesterday while I stood, still innocent, in my mother's kitchen, watching him at dawn.

I struggled to get to my feet and Alecto's hand reached through the rib and grabbed my shoulder. His eyes like lamps stared without expression. He jerked me back toward him and I still could not scream, my voice severed from my body. I watched his mouth open, blood dripping down his nose like thick tears. And then, disbelieving, I heard the furious voice that was his.

"You'll rot."

He tried to squeeze his own body at mine through the bones and, shocked by his sinuous rage, with a sudden twist and jerk I cracked his wrist against a rib and pulled my hand free. Then I scrambled away and escaped across that open field. The spring mud sucked the boot off my swollen heel and when I glanced back, Alecto had picked himself up and was nursing his wrist against his body.

I still fled though there was no need now. I was an absurd and fallen creature, one boot off and one on, limping, running. I didn't stop until I got back to my mother's house. And Alecto, finished with his carcass of an elephant, disappeared in uncouth passage.

QUID PETIS?

(What do you ask?)

The elephants went to the place where Lear fell and stood all day scenting the earth. Three full days they stood there, digging up chips of bone, bits of hair, burying their trunks in the blood-soaked field. I sat watching them from the fence. Gradually they strayed from the spot, moving along the fences and coming back to walk in their great pacing circle. I brought their food outside after a few days and put it in the far corner of the back field so they would have a reason to leave the place.

Jo was flown to Florida. I could not persuade him to stay. Alecto disappeared. Day after day I sat on the fence watching the elephants and aching. My baby kicked and turned upside-down in the waters and I curled around my own stomach.

When a monk enters a monastery he must answer a question from the community. They chant to him, "What do you ask?" and the monk answers, "Mercy."

But I was alone in a place without chanting. The elephants

rumbled only to each other their customary greetings. At bathtime, feeding time, and shackled up for the night, they swayed restlessly, scenting at the door of the barn and at Jo's bed. I went about his tasks as best I could. They tolerated my inexperienced hands and my inability to understand the subtle language they had with Jo. *They'll teach you what you need to know,* he'd said. I turned to Kezia to show me, to show the others to listen to me. I was in her power as she was in mine. I stroked her trunk and leaned on her, day after day. At night I could smell elephant all over me.

The Safari directors put me in charge of the elephants and asked me to do Jo's work. I told them I didn't know enough, didn't want so much work, couldn't do it, but they shook their heads and said, "There is no one else." I couldn't submit and I couldn't leave and I couldn't die. There were elephants hungry and needing exercise. There was Kezia, pregnant, and the Safari would open soon. I didn't know all I needed to know to take care of them. Slowly Kezia accepted me as her keeper and I felt her wondering, *What do you ask?* I often didn't know what to answer but I pretended. I want you not to hurt me. I want you not to kill me. I want you to hold your foot ready to work on. I want you to walk out into the elephant yard with me. I want you to stand while I bathe you. I want you to eat and to sleep. I want you to allow me to put the howdah on you, to bear weight, to raise your trunk, to walk beside me and safely carry small children. She had the power to do all these things. When I was too tired to go on I stood among them

and felt their graceful acceptance of a life they had not chosen. I made our daily routine as simple as I could. More and
more I recorded their silence, took the tapes back to my
mother's house and when she was sleeping I listened to
their low rumbles. One afternoon while I recorded, not
knowing if they were speaking or quiet in the dark barn, I
whispered to them, "What do you want?" And on the tape
I heard for the first time the lowest of all their calls,
aaaaaaaaaaaa, a sound I have come to understand as *mercy.*

ELEPHANT-ENGLISH
DICTIONARY
PART FOUR

Nurturing

After survival, the single most important concern of female elephants is the care and nurturing of the young. Elephant, more than many languages, has specific nurturing utterances, everything from lullabies to "Don't bother me now, dear." They are uttered by all members of the group. A rite of passage for a seven- or eight-year-old female comes when she stops hearing such language directed at her and begins to use it herself. I have heard elephants as young as three and four begin to verbalize nurturing language and I consider it a sign of great emotional and intellectual health.

A Note on Vocabulary: Elephant Pi Factor

There are 52 Prime Utterances in Elephant, by which I mean sounds that cannot be broken down any further. The feature in the language that counterbalances this small vocabulary is the Pi Factor. Elephant discourse, similar to pi, expands without settling into predictable patterns. It remains comprehensible but not repetitive, altered by rhythm, and context. Because the language is strongly oriented toward communal expression, any individual's utterance may be joined at any time in unison, harmony, counterpoint, and finally (though rarely) in interruption. This makes the vocabulary more rich than the identification of 52 Prime Utterances might at first suggest.

aah: (18-20 Hz.) A birthing chant, made during the delivery and after the baby is born. The more inexperienced the mother, the longer the chant.

One of the things I am proudest of at the Safari is our live births. Each of our females has given birth, with the exception of Gertrude, who shows no interest in mating.

After a stillbirth in my first months at the Safari, I decided to allow the other elephants to act as midwives when a baby was being born. Since that time, I have never lost a baby. I think that the necessary presence of others at the birth is indicated by the steady chanting that takes place after the event. The elephants encourage the newborn to stand with their trunks and with songs *(see erh)*.

Analogies might be made to parts of the world where women gather round each other after a birth and rub the mother's skin with sweet oils, swaddle and hold and sing to the new baby. No sooner is a child born than they are touching the child with hands and voices, gathering the new mother and her baby back into their community after the dangerous voyage out.

Elephants honour life by placing enormous emphasis on the rearing of the young. This is a central emotional and social point of the community's organization.

erh: (35+ Hz.) *Try!*

An encouraging call to a baby to do something. It is used immediately after birth to get the newborn to stand up, accompanied by help with the trunk. It is the first utterance a baby elephant hears, and it continues frequently through the first few months of life, as the baby is urged to wait, to run, to swim, to climb, to try any of the "firsts" of life.

huuuaaarrr: (35 Hz.) Soothing sound for babies under three years of age.

This chant functions as a lullaby when a small elephant rests under her mother. I once heard Gertrude chanting it to Saba with an element of traditional Mother Goose irony, as in "Mother, may I go out to swim? Yes, my darling daughter. Hang your clothes on a hickory limb, But don't go near the water!"

I have also heard *huuuaaarrr oooaaarrr,* a song sung together by our entire group of elephants after Kezia's first live birth, when her baby slept for the first time. Moving and lovely, it was a celebration of the mother as much as the baby, a celebration of all of them for the new life in their midst.

tchr bra ow: (23 Hz.) *Stop bothering me with silliness.*

Young elephants are playful and inquisitive. This tender dodge is uttered when the mothers or aunts have had enough of the young elephants and wish to distract them from, in effect, asking too many questions.

bra bra: (25 Hz.) Discipline sound meaning "Don't do that," often accompanied by a restraining gesture of the trunk.

A fundamental principle in the rearing of any species is the knowledge that the young will copy in minute detail everything the adults do. Elephant socialization is based on this idea, encouraging behaviour that fits in with the group while tolerating youthful curiosity and exuberance. However, when a small elephant persists in an activity that endangers herself or the group, a mother or auntie does not hesitate to stop the behaviour. For example, when Saba was very young, she had a dangerous inclination to slip under the fence. Unwittingly, she'd wander off after a scent in the air. For several days I watched Alice gently tug her back with her trunk. But when the young one kept forgetting, Alice finally uttered a frightening bra and pulled her back sharply.

eeeeaaa^: (120–240 Hz.) Panic scream, strongest of all elephant calls, used when a female is rushing to help a baby in danger.

Second in importance to nurturing the young is the begetting of them. Mating is a highly ritualized, communal activity. Females sing estrus songs lasting up to forty-five minutes, and after, they sing post-copulatory songs. I have hesitated to mention the possibility of an erotic component in Elephant, although I feel it is present in these haunting chants. In the wild, males stay with a female for several days, guarding her against the intrusion of other males and mating frequently. Even though the mating elephants at the Ontario Safari are protected from danger, males and females still sing these songs, which are a necessary part of the mating ritual.

mrow mrooo mroow mroooah: (14 Hz.) Estrus call.

This is a remarkable, throbbing chant, usually a deep rumble that becomes stronger and higher in pitch before sinking down again. In the wild, it is thought to function as a locator for roving males.

When I hear this gorgeous prelude to mating I am reminded of a Beethoven cello solo.

brrr rrr oh: (14-20 Hz.) A very low call denoting support of mating.

This is generally sung by a group of females in overlapping spondaic and trochaic rhythms during mating. It creates a passionate effect similar to that of "The Song of Solomon," to honour the ineluctable mystery and to remind the mating elephant she has a witness.

oar^oar: (25 Hz.) Post-copulatory estrous sequence.

Two or more quite intense shouts indicating ending of mating cycle.

^rraaarr ^rraaaarr: (40–55 Hz.) Threat call of a male in musth.

This is often accompanied by strong territorial gestures of charges (mock or real) and banging of tusks. In captivity it is directed toward a keeper, or a tree.

~rrowr: (60–120 Hz.) Musth song of male after he has mated and stands protecting the female, awaiting the next opportunity to mate.

A male continues this call intermittently throughout the mating period. It is meant to ward off other males who approach and is repeated strongly when he gives himself over to the bewildering minute. It may also serve as a kind of reassurance to his partner that he is protecting her, although the real protection is provided by the group of females looking on.

KEZIA

I was finally empty. Jo was gone. When his jaw was un-wired he called from his brother's trailer in Florida and said he wasn't coming back.

"Jo, you have to come back."

"I can't."

"What about Kezia?" What about me?

"I got a new job down here, Sophie. As soon as I'm on my feet again."

"I'll help, Jo. You've got to come. They need you."

"It's too big an operation. I've got a nice little zoo here. Two Asian elephants. No breeding. No males. I'm tired of the north. I'm tired of the circuses."

"It will catch up with you . . . Jo?" I was talking into silence.

"Are you all right?"

"Yes. Jo, there was nothing you could do. Lear was getting too old. He had arthritis." I couldn't feel him over the telephone.

Finally he said, "Where's Alecto?"

"He's gone."

"There'll be a paper on Lear someday."

"I suppose. I don't think he'll be back."

"Don't be so sure."

"I think he's run his course. I told the Safari if they wanted me to stay he couldn't come back."

I felt him stiffen, "How's Kezia?"

"She seems fine so far."

I buried Alecto deep and deeper. My eyes opened and battered, I divined the life before me. The elephants had to be taken care of. My baby was dropping toward the world. And I had to see my mother through her dying.

The only solution to her constant pain was her own end. There was no skin left between us, the air was raw as the open flesh of a burn.

"Sophie, what's going to happen to the birds when I die?"

"What makes you worry about the birds?"

"What else would I worry about?" she said. "The birds will still be here. Someone has to take care of them."

I didn't want her to talk about it. I wanted her to say, "I'm not going to die." She waited and said nothing.

"I'll take care of your birds."

"But you'll be busy with your new baby. I know how the first few months are. Will you live here? I know you won't want them flying around. I suppose you could put them in the cage. Moore would hate it. Maybe you could just leave Moore out and keep the rest locked up?"

She seemed hopeful about this and I nodded.

"I was going to build an aviary outside this spring. Beside my studio."

"Maybe I could."

"I wish I could have been here for your baby, Sophie. You mustn't be too sad. A baby can feel it. I would have loved her. You must love her to bits. It's all for such a short time."

I didn't go to the Safari that day. I crawled up on my mother's bed instead. She tried to tell me what she knew about mothering, a thousand seeds tossed into the air. She tried to tell me all the things that would have unfolded slowly between us as my baby grew and we watched her together. She said the most important thing to know is that a child wants to be just like you.

She said, "Give her everything and all of yourself and make sure you keep some back for yourself and do your own work too."

"A pragmatist!"

"It's never easy. The paradox is that a child takes everything and gives everything. You have to do that back. But you can't do it well unless you have something of your own. There's enough. Give all of it. It drives you crazy but do it. There," she said, waving her hand in front of her, "there's my two cents' worth!"

I thought of her sweaters. She didn't find them until I had been away many years.

"You didn't get to your real work until after I was gone."

She took my hands and said, "It is all real work, and I couldn't have found the sweaters without you. A lot of them are yours."

She reached for her glass and I handed it to her. She took a sip of plain water and then she pulled herself a little straighter on the bed. "And you'll always miss her more than she misses you."

I laughed and went to make tea. When I came back I said, "I never knew your stomach is so hard when you're pregnant."

"You've felt her move?"

"Of course, I'm five months."

"I always forget the dates."

"What do you remember?"

"I remember the wonderful shape. I remember everyone wanting to touch me. There was a pencil-seller who used to hang around the café below our apartment. He was a dwarf, with crossed eyes and he wore glasses. I'd give him a few francs sometimes. One morning he walked straight up to me, stuck out his hand and rubbed it on my stomach."

"How awful."

"It was . . ." Her eyes drifted to the back of the room. "There was another night, when your father and I went out to see friends in the Bois de Boulogne. I was happy to get out of our tiny room. After dinner we were all sitting together and my friend asked me if she could touch my stomach. She said, 'I love that feeling.' I didn't mind, her voice was so soft, and she placed her large hands on my stomach. After a moment she slipped them under my shirt. They were warm and light, and her two little girls came running into the room and asked what we were doing. She asked if they could touch too. I was sitting on a stool and your father had moved over and was standing so I could lean on him. The older girl touched like her mother, gently placing her hands and waiting, and the little girl had a much firmer touch, moving, searching. I think she felt the baby first. She said, 'It bumped!' and they all laughed lightly together with her. The woman said to her two daughters, *'C'est tellement beau . . . non?'* It made me feel dizzy, kind of faint . . ." She smiled. "But when you're pregnant you always feel a bit faint, don't you."

"That you may learn to bear the beams of love . . ."

"Yes," she said leaning back, "it is very intense, isn't it?"

I moved closer to her then and took one of her hands and put it on my hard, rounded stomach under my sweater. Her hands, though still young, were heavily veined and thin, muscular from her years of gardens and stretching canvases and playing piano. They were cool at first, then they warmed on my body and she placed them firmly and moved them slowly. The slash of pain between her eyebrows relaxed as she searched to touch my baby. Her breathing was shallow and laboured even with the oxygen tubes in. I think I felt the baby move, I wasn't sure, and after a long time she said under her breath, "There . . ." Then she took her hands away and pulled my sweater back down gently and said, "Don't you feel you're the first one in the world? I did."

"Yes, I do sometimes."

━━━◆◆◆━━━

For one week before Kezia's baby was due, I slept in the barn. Each morning when I awoke on my haysweet cot, I'd slip out from under the blankets and shiver into yesterday's pants and tatty grey sweater. The elephants all stirred and rumbled and stretched together, some slow waking, others awake and waiting in the darkness. No one was ever left out and all moved together into each particular dawn, their purpose simply to be, and to be together. They began their mornings by touching, the tips of their trunks exploring each other's mouths and genitals and faces, swaying like seaweed in a fresh morning current. Ever since I'd been at the Safari Kezia had been practising her mothering on Saba. She'd muscle in and stand over Saba. Once when Alice wouldn't move, the two of them stood jostling each other, their trunks held out side by side over the sleeping baby like an awning. I had even seen Kezia reach her trunk to Alice's breasts, take a dab of milk and put it on her own breast.

Winter came twice that year. The earth had been wet and fragrant and then there was a spring snowstorm. Chickadees tucked themselves against frozen tree trunks and curled their heads under plumped-up wings. I carried big pockets of seed to toss over the crusty ice for them. I was tired all the time. I took to staring at tiny things, single crystals of snow, each six-sided and each different. Or so they say. Who would know? I dug down into a snowbank with a stick and saw an unscanned poem—depth hoar and corn snow and ice skeletons hung on rimed particles and lump groupels and dendritic crystals, needles and branches, layers of days of snow.

I slept in the barn because Jo always said Kezia needed to know we would be there for the birth. I had been trying to let her know I wouldn't leave. I had a night nurse in for my mother, and she was excited too.

"How many chances do you get to see an elephant born?" she said. "If I were well enough, I'd come too. See if you can get some pictures."

I awoke to Kezia swaying and turning, the others gathered in a half-circle around her. Once it started the baby came quickly. The floor was awash in fluid and I saw the head crown. In another few seconds the whole baby fell, whoosh, to the floor and I quickly spread bags of sawdust around its feet for traction. The first thing a wild baby elephant has to do is get to its feet, but babies born inside, in captivity, slip and slide on their own birth waters. There was a terrible, dead stillness to the perfectly shaped tiny elephant lying between Kezia's legs. I watched as Kezia tried to lift it up. She wrapped her trunk under it and lifted. She tried to raise the head, to stretch out the front legs, to lift under the stomach. She nudged at her baby's sides. But there was nothing. I left the stillborn with her for an hour. All through that hour she never stopped trying to lift it to its feet.

I had radioed some of the other keepers to come and help. They wanted to take it away immediately, but I made them stay back. "Let her know it's dead," I snarled at them. "She needs to know."

The other elephants in the big stall were all reaching their trunks toward her. In the silence of the barn I could feel the pressures changing and I knew they were chanting to her. Finally I shackled Kezia's leg and the trainers heaved and pushed the slippery two hundred and fifty pound baby onto a burlap sheet and dragged it outside. In that moment, exhausted, I felt my baby fluttering inside, sorrow and hope wrapped around each other like the overlapping folds of an elephant's hide.

I stayed in the barn with Kezia after they'd taken the stillborn out. I put her in the big stall with the others and they came to her and touched her with their trunks. I fell asleep uneasily, sinking into my own heavy fatigue, and I hoped Kezia could rest too. The tiredness I felt when I was pregnant was a thick cocoon. I cried most nights for Jo and for my mother but I never lay sleepless and I never woke in the middle of the night. I could no longer smell Jo in the barn cot. I cried now for Kezia's baby and then slept sleep thick with dreams.

Before dawn I was woken by a feeling of absence and when I roused myself and lay listening I realized I couldn't hear them all. I rolled to my side to get up, looked over at the elephants and saw that Kezia was gone. She'd unshackled herself and managed to get out the barn door. Quickly

I pulled on my barn clothes and ran outside. Her fresh prints were not pointed toward the elephant fields or the maples but away, toward the Safari entrance, toward the road. Breathing heavily, I trotted through the front gate where the lock had been easily broken.

I slowed to a fast walk, following her prints, and through the darkness I finally saw her body, swaying down the road where horse farms and vegetable farms were strung like beads through the fields. She walked slowly and alone on that dark country road as if she were memorizing something. Drops of milk hung frozen from her breasts. I got closer and closer and I was afraid I'd startle her, she'd hurt me, she'd run to the highway. I was afraid now of rifles, of officials, of how things look, of how they are. I heard her rumbling, *Onrrrrarrrr, Onrrrrarrrrr* . . .

I had nothing but my barn mitts, not even a stick, and I'd never been outside the Safari gates with an elephant. The fields rolled to the horizon like lumpy dough. The road behind was broken with drifts of snow. I had to talk to her, soothe her, relieve her painful breasts.

I heard Kezia paunsing, *Onrrrrarrrrr* . . .

"Easy, Kezia. Easy girl," I purred, as low as I could.

I knew she would do anything for me if I could help her achieve her purpose. But tonight her purpose was to nurture and I could not give her her baby back. And so, I asked her to take care of me. I leaned on her the way I often did when we were walking and I got tired. I put out my arm for her to hook her trunk under and I waited. After an infinite five seconds, she reached out, hooked her trunk around my arm, slowly turned and began to lead me home. Salt tears stinging on my cheeks, Kezia led me back down the road toward the barns, past the vegetable fields, the horse farms, my mother's house. Her bedroom light was on.

I stopped only once on that long slow walk home and Kezia patiently waited. I stopped to break a pine bough to brush away our tracks around the gates. I hoped the sun would melt all the rest away. The thin dawn taped itself like a piece of old and yellowing cellophane to the horizon and the cold adhered to my skin. Kezia moved forward steadily now, and I stayed with her. Everything was sticking to us, as if a box of ashes had spilled open and was swirling around us in the wind before we could get it buried.

PASSIO

"I loved summers best," my mother said. "I remember how the small muscles in your legs grew harder each spring. You liked to lift up the moss on the rocks and look for these tiny little red ants. We had good warbler migrations in those days and we'd sit together under the fir trees when they passed through and you always pretended you were in a tent. We made small fires in the evening behind the house. You were a wonderful child to spend time with."

As she remembered, I remembered too. I had loved our old farmhouses, the pencil lines up the doorjambs marking my height, the smell of her paints in various lofts and back porches and tiny rooms. I remembered playing boat on the stairs and the smell of ironed cotton. I remembered learning to exchange looks with my mother. She wanted me with her and she wanted me to laugh at what she laughed at. The days were busy with school and her teaching and her work. One day I threw paint all over her studio to try to get her to stop working.

But there were always stories at night, adventures of children with brothers and sisters, tales of animals who talked and travelled on planes, rhymes with strange and wonderful Saxon words: niggeldy, noddeldy, patching a cob and riding a gig, coaches drawn by dapples and greys and little girls eating curds and whey, loobedy-loo and loobedy-light, puppies with pockets, tinkers and vintners and mackerel-skies, sabbath children bonny and blithe, parsons and joiners and cobblers and hosiers, tuffets and bong-trees and runcible spoons, half a pound of tuppenny treacle, and silvery, smiling, invisible moons, words chanted and lollopped on our tongues, and one day, "Rigadoon, rigadoon, now let her fly, sit her on father's foot, jump her up high," and I asked out of the blue, "Where is my father?"

But she only laughed lightly and said, "Oh, he's in France, we'll see him one day soon," and then she tried to make me laugh, tickling and chanting,

Once there was an elephant
Who tried to use the telephant—
No! No! I mean an elephone
Who tried to use the telephone.

In the last few days she lay very still on the bed. She slept wearing the oxygen tubes and when I gave her the bedpan I had to be very careful because her skin bruised so easily. But as I moved around her bed in the daytime I sometimes made her smile by chanting the nonsense rhymes she'd chanted to me when she was still the mother and I was still the small girl in a hurry to grow older.

The evenings were long as she dozed in and out. My baby had turned head down and I felt that achey stretching between my pubis and my belly button as the life inside me lengthened toward breath. Though I was much alone, strange to say, I was not lonely. I moved a big card table into her room and spread out my work on elephant language. Each evening, when she fell asleep, I took solace in the work. I surveyed the tangle of tapes and notes of elephant sounds, dumped the big brown box on the table, took my mother's transcription notes and labelled and sorted. I listened and refined the transcriptions and interpreted and made lists of inaudible sound. Hour after hour I cross-referenced and indexed. I sat before the stack of work to be done each night, my bones and spirit too craven to even begin, and stopped thinking so I could work. I think that work saved me.

I had recorded elephant language much impaired by my own deafness. My tapes were sometimes long, sometimes brief. My notes were scribbled on scraps of paper covered with drawings, dates and hasty descriptions along the margins. They were cluttered with first impressions about Jo and my pregnancy and my mother and Alecto. My mother's transcriptions were neatly folded under an elastic band around each tape box. Painstakingly she had charted the patterns she'd found in their chanting.

Now came the great discipline—not of love, which

demands will and desire to attend to another, but of work, which demands the other to wait. There was a tedium to it, comparing, deciphering and organizing. Whenever a recording seemed too shapeless, whenever I felt too distracted, I made myself submit, made myself accept that there are patterns that I did not yet understand.

I gave myself to the discipline, to listening without judgment. My heart and mind opened to the sounds. Elephant is not a language of one to another, question and answer, proposition and counter-argument. It is a language of chanting, communal sound looking for shifting communal sense. I sat beside my mother as she slipped away and I worked. I listened to the elephants' low rumbling and, lulled by their incomprehensible songs, I sometimes felt as though I were seeing into the place where the light of dead stars is born.

———◆———

The last afternoon, when I came in from the barn, she was calling out in a panicky voice, "Sophie, Sophie, I'm so glad you're back."

A new and very young day nurse was at the door, eager to leave. She reported tersely that my mother had had a difficult day. "She wouldn't sit up," she complained. "I got her up and she kept trying to lie down."

"For God's sake let her lie down then," I snapped and sent her away. When I rounded the familiar corner into my mother's bedroom, Moore dove past my head. If I ever got my hands on him I'd flush him down the toilet. Everything was knocked off her table. Her pitcher lay cracked on the floor and water was spilled on the corner of the bed and soaked into the sheets. The room smelled of urine.

"Sophie, I'm so thirsty. That woman was awful, I sent her out."

I saw her dry lips and went into the kitchen for ice chips and another pitcher. I put water and a straw in a clean glass, held her head up a little and touched the water to her lips.

She looked into my eyes and said, "Sophie, I'm sorry, I'm so glad you're back . . ."

I rolled her gently to the side, each movement ragging at the pain in her body. I slipped off the sheets and the plastic bed sheet and with a warm cloth washed her body and put on the new sheets and a fresh gown, moving her as little as possible. I went into the kitchen and got a broom and dustpan and cleaned up the broken pitcher, lifting the smaller shards of glass out of the carpet with my fingers. I picked up the things from her table. As I was finished, her poor body exploded again and I began it all over, cleaning and changing the sheets, pulling at the edges, trying to get her comfortable. I washed her from behind as much as I could and she said, "There isn't much dignity at the end, you give up on that."

"It's all right, I'm not looking."

"The hell you're not."

I took all the laundry and stuffed it in the basement, and

by the time I was back upstairs she was moaning and wet with sweat. "Open the window, open the window, I need air."

"Mom, what about the birds?"

"Please Sophie, I need air."

I got most of them into the aviary by shaking the seed box. Moore stayed up high on her curtain rod and wouldn't come down even for food. I struggled and banged at the window to get it open, just a crack, hoping Moore couldn't squeeze through. When it finally jerked open, I could smell the turned-over spring earth of the vegetable fields. I gave her her night morphine pill and I sat next to her, waiting for it to soothe her, stroking her hands. After a while, eyelids heavy and drugged, she fell asleep.

I moved off the bed and went to my table, put on the headphones to listen to the elephant tapes and fell asleep folded forward. I woke up to her groaning in the middle of the night and I rolled heavily up, my neck stiff, the headphones falling off to the floor. Half asleep I stood beside her bed.

"Sophie, please," she said. "Do something."

I tried to put a cool, wet cloth to her lips but she writhed wildly side to side and cried, "Please, give me something."

It was very early in the morning and there were hours until her next tablet. I looked at her eyes so desperate with the pain and I went into the bathroom to get some of the morphine in her medicine box. Carefully I uncapped a needle, snapped open the glass vial, put the needle tip into the vial. I pulled back the plunger, gently tipping the liquid toward the end of the needle to keep the seal. Deft now, I could empty the tiny bottles completely. I held the needle up, tapped two bubbles to the top and nudged the plunger up until a drop of the precious stuff pushed through the hole. Then, squeezing a bit of flesh on the back of her arm, quickly I slid the needle in at an angle, pulled back the plunger to check for blood and pushed in the morphine. I could not bear the idea of hurting her any more. She seemed to settle a little. I watched as the morphine melted through her body. I leaned back in my chair beside her hoping for a moment's respite, thinking this round was over, but in a few minutes she was awake again, her face twisted in panic. She held the oxygen tubes at her chin as if she didn't know whether to rip them out or push them further in. "Sophie, I can't breathe, you've got to do something."

For the first time in all those months my stomach froze in fear. I thought this might be another, still worse part of the dying. I didn't know how much pain she could bear or what more I could do. I fixed her oxygen tubes and held ice chips in a cloth for her to suck, and after she got back her breath, she stopped a moment and said, "I love you, Sophie."

She rested back and the panic of suffocation subsided. She rasped shallowly into the room and I couldn't make out what she was saying. She writhed and struggled to breathe. The awful gurgling air filled the silence and she rasped, "Do something, please, you've got to do something."

I couldn't do this alone, I didn't know what this was. I

ran to the telephone to call for an ambulance, but I dropped the receiver because she was screaming, "Don't leave!"

I ran to her box in the bathroom and took out the extra bottles of morphine and, shaking, prepared another injection. I pushed it through her bruises and she settled, but in minutes she was writhing again and I couldn't bear her so far away from me wrapped up and carried away in pain. She wasn't finished, there were things left to do. I broke another bottle of morphine and she groaned and thrashed. She couldn't get any air. She was drowning in her own lungs. She lifted her head and dropped it horribly and I filled another needle and gave her more. I saw Moore fussing near the open window but my mother was calling wildly, and before I could do anything he squeezed himself out through the crack and was gone. I thought, "How can I tell her?" and was going to phone an ambulance again when she half screamed, "Enough, do something, Sophie!" but I didn't know what to do. I was afraid to give her more. There was only one more left. I could give her the next pill. How many injections had I given her?

Her body stopped thrashing but her eyes stilled and stared at mine. She breathed, gurgling and rasping, then stopped. I waited, holding my breath. I thought she was dead. I felt for her pulse and jumped when she heaved in another shuddering breath. She stopped again and then suddenly sucked in more air. I held her hand and she stopped breathing then suddenly sucked in another breath. She stopped breathing and with these awful wheezes she breathed again, and each time I waited until finally she didn't breathe in again, not ever again.

———•◦•———

Elephant breath is a tonic. If you have a headache the best thing in the world is to stand quietly with an elephant, its trunk in your mouth. After they took away my mother's body, I couldn't bear to be alone and I left the house and walked across the field wondering what to do now, looking through the darkness at the peaceful white fences of the horse farms, the spirit shapes of snowdrifts in the fields.

There are moments we get stuck in, tell over and over until time softens them. That night I could not be alone. The death thrashing was over but I could not admit it. I walked around the outside of the barns, once, twice, three times, and when I decided to go through the door Kezia was awake and waiting for me. She raised her trunk in greeting, stood listening in the darkness and then gently lowered her trunk and blew lightly on my face. I stopped crying, petted her cheeks and delicately she slipped her trunk inside my mouth and we breathed together, her gentle finger rubbing lightly along the inside of my gums. Her trunk was large and damp and I opened my mouth wide. She stood breathing into me a long time that night. It felt like a kiss and a greeting, I did not know from where.

———•◦•———

My mother had time to plan her memorial service. And since there was only me for family I suspect it was planned for me. Our last party, in a way. She wanted Arvo Pärt's *Passio* played in full. She wanted the minister to commend her spirit to God. And that was it.

I sat alone in the front row of the crematorium listening for seventy minutes and fifty-two seconds to her favourite recording of the dark ebb and flow of Pärt's interpretation of John's Passion. The chorus and organ in a slow descent announced *Passio Domini nostri Jesu Christi secundum Joannem* and I settled in to listen. Pärt's layered chorus unwound the story of the long walk to the cross. I was relieved to hear the familiar voices. In a little while all those people behind me would stand with me and walk out of the old stone building and then it would be over. With my large pregnant belly I would walk out with them and then I would go back to her house and she would not be there in her bed filling the place with her loud music and her conversation. But for this last moment, her music still filled me.

— You're alone now.

— There are the elephants . . .

— She never felt alone either. She loved you to bits.

— To crumbs.

— To blades of grass.

— To grains of sand.

— More than everything.

The music pierced the numbness with aching; she had loved this music and she could not hear it. If something is

188

unbearable I set it down. This time I could not set down what I couldn't bear. Listening to the music she so loved I was struck back into awful chaos by a thought I still think often: how she would have loved this.

I had always wondered why Pärt chose John's telling of the crucifixion. I had said once to my mother, "He should have chosen one of the more dramatic gospels. It makes Christ so much more human to hear him cry out his doubt."

"By that point he's almost done with this world anyway."

"But the torture made him doubt. I wonder why John left it out."

"Perhaps he just assumed the doubt. Doubt is the centre, like the grit in the pearl. It doesn't much matter if you cry it out or not. It's the same with everything. Don't you have that feeling with your elephants? Isn't there always a kernel of doubt that the imagined life between you isn't the same for them as for you? That you don't fully understand? But you don't cry out. You just keep working at it until you understand a little better."

There were so many things she said. How to remember all the stories? But if they were written every one ... I suppose that even the world itself could not contain the books that should be written.

I watched the minister rise and descend the two steps to stand behind the coffin. The people in the crematorium stirred back to life out of their solitary meditations, anxious now to go out into the weak spring light. Christ's voice sang *Ecce mater tua,* Behold your mother.

Why had she wished me to sit and listen to this after she was no longer living, my mother, the woman who dying asked me only for breath? The voices fell low and lower. The chorus moaned and soared and sank again and finally we heard the last ... *miserere nobis. Amen.*

Death was come, nature's purpose fulfilled. The music was finished and men moved to each side of her coffin. The minister broke the silence, her human voice too sullied to speak after the bells and timpanies and strings. But she spoke because her work was to break the silence, she spoke the simple words my mother had asked for. She intoned over the coffin, "I commend your spirit to God."

And then, according to my mother's wishes, the men slid her into the fire and I drowned in salt waters as her dead body burned.

ELEPHANT-ENGLISH
DICTIONARY
PART FIVE

Expletives

This is my favourite category of speech act, rich and varied. While there is no such thing as a profanity in Elephant because the sacred and the profane are not separate, there are many expressions of exasperation, disgust, surprise, pleasure. The general nature of a contented elephant is inquisitive, witty, creative and full of *joie de vivre*. Expletives help an elephant express her complex nature.

In most studies of dead and unwritten languages, expletives tend to be relegated by the dictionary-makers to a class of sounds used primarily to modulate rhythm. But in Elephant, they contribute mightily to meaning, are stylistically and syntactically important and often signal mood changes and shifts in the direction of the discourse.

I include as many expletives as I have found, fully recognizing the danger of this enterprise because the nature of expletives is primarily creative and changeable to a degree unknown to other categories of vocabulary.

A Note About Metaphors and Expletives

Buried in human language is a continual and subtle shifting between the naming of a thing and its metaphorical significance. In Chinese, for example, a greeting as conventional as the English, "Hello, how are you?" is "Ni hao, ni chiguo le ma?" or "Hello, have you eaten yet?" The reference to eating is a metaphor for the state of well-being. Learning the metaphors of a culture is a way into the culture's deep structures.

Since Elephant concerns itself not with naming but with being, its buried metaphors tend to concern states of being. The utterances for food and water are sometimes buried in situations concerning other pleasures. Expletives also express the level of well-being not only for the individual but also for the group. They create a backbone of feeling that unites the group.

tchrp: (130 Hz. Squeak through trunk) *How curious! And pleasureful.*

Upon seeing something unusual an elephant will squeak. When a piece of string was left in the yard, the group came up to it, *tchrp*'ed, then picked it up, tossed it around and played with it.

brooh: (92 Hz. Exhaled snort through trunk) *How stupid!* Displeasure.

An expression of dismay.

rii: (18–26 Hz). Pleasure.

This utterance can be combined with others to express either simple pleasure or a kind of elephant laughter at witty or humorous behaviour. *(See poor^rrr,* food; and *owrr~rrr,* water)

wht wht: (340 Hz. Whistle) Astonished pleasure.

When Saba was young she liked to whistle when she got special foods. As she was learning the Elephant songs and chants she liked to insert this favourite expletive. She'd begin the community song then break off in exuberance. She reminded me of Praxilla of Sicyon, who was cited by the men of her day as an example of how not to write poetry. I suspect this was because she couldn't help throwing in her own pleasures and preoccupations, as in this fragment from her hymn, "To Adonis, Dying":

Loveliest of what I leave
is the sun himself
Next to that the bright stars
and the face of mother moon
Oh yes, and cucumbers in season,
and apples, and pears.

Saba's first songs were a little like this:

~ah ~ah oooo ~ah ~ah
~~~pra ^wht wht

freely translated:

Praise the morning, praise all of us together.
Praise our being together apart.
Praise us. Praise the light.
Hey! I'm hungry! Where's something good to eat?

pft: (40+ Hz. Air blown roughly through trunk) A note
of light frustration when a task can't be accomplished,
usually a task imposed from outside.

trt trt: (137 Hz. Between a whistle and an exhaled, high-
pitched snort) *Mind your own business* (mild threat
implied), *I know what I'm doing.*

I heard this after moving my piano into the barn during
the winter to give the elephants something to do. One
morning I came in and found all the keys ripped off. It
turned out that Gertrude had taken and buried them
behind a loose board. (The piano was old and the keys were
ivory. I do not know if this had any bearing on the event.)

errh: (30-35 Hz. Repeated grunt) *Um . . . um . . . hmmm.*
A memory grunt. This is one of the few expletives
that is infrasonic.

I have heard this utterance in several contexts, usually
having to do with the physical and mental effort required
to remember something. 1. Alice trying to turn on a water
tap she'd turned on before (that I'd locked differently).

2. Kezia playing with mud and leaves just before creating a little hat to put on her head on an exceptionally hot August day.

noo^orrr^noo^orrr^noo: (12-15 Hz.) Despair, sob-like
  futility uttered over and over in a trochaic chant.

I include this little chant in its entirety because it was one of the few I ever heard by a male. It was uttered by Lear when he was frustrated with his training. He was asked to do something he simply didn't understand and finally he lay on his side, let tears fall from his eyes and made this song.

wff: (10-12 Hz.) Utterance of appreciation made when a
  young elephant creates a meaningful new chant.

tttttttt: (50 Hz. spitting-like click) Ironic doubt.

I call this the "Mass for Holy Saturday" expletive: *O felix culpa quae talem ac tantum meruit habere redemptorum* (O blessed sin rewarded by so good and so great a redeemer). It is a small sound uttered when an elephant transgresses the order of the Safari but discovers through the transgression a larger truth, rather like Milton's Adam.

> Full of doubt I stand,
> Whether I should repent me now of sin
> By me done and occasioned, or rejoice
> Much more, that much more good thereof shall spring,

To God more glory, more good will to men
From God, and over wrath grace shall abound.

I have seen Gertrude, sporting the double face of irony,
after breaking into the grain bin, look at me and murmur
tttttttt, "Full of doubt I stand ..."

The BIRTH *of* OMEGA, or
BREEDING in CAPTIVITY

Elephants have a system of mothering that, typically, has little to do with ownership. Generally, elephant babies are not more than a few feet from their mothers for the first three years of life. Other females join in the mothering, especially young females, eight, nine, ten years old. A peaceful community spends its days following the rhythms of the youngest of the group. If a baby is sleeping (most often in the shade underneath its mother) the whole group stops and waits until it awakens.

In the final months of my pregnancy I felt a desire to burrow and a craving to sleep. Sleep was the other life, of things growing unseen. I slept everywhere. In the barn. Out back in the fields. In the bathroom. There was nothing better than to tumble into sleep, awake refreshed, eat, and lie down again. But I needed to get things organized for the elephants. Bring in a temporary keeper. I had to take the Grays back to the Safari and get the budgies used to spending more time in their aviary. I had to do legal and banking and gallery

paperwork for my mother. And figure out how I was going to manage things when the baby came.

Our culture doesn't encourage us to sleep.

I spent most nights in the barn. The elephants liked having me there and I felt better among them in the small cot than alone in the empty house. Having no place I had to be, and no person who cared where I was, I began to slip into the daily rhythm that the elephants preferred. They slept most deeply in the smallest hours then roused themselves and liked to walk out in the fields just before dawn. I walked out with them to watch the sunrise each day, dozed in the late mornings and fell asleep early in the evening. I didn't do their feet every day and I didn't always bathe them as the days grew longer. I relaxed the strict routine we'd always had and they didn't object or become unruly. With all of our obligations to the world dissolved, we wandered behind the fences and ate and slept when we wanted to. It was a time of great contentment among them, simple unfolding timeless days. Even Kezia began to waggle her ears again and nudge Alice aside for a chance to spoil Saba.

One early morning I was out back watching the elephants toss fallen leaves under the bones of a dew-shrouded maple tree. Their great bodies rubbed against each other, ribs expanding with deep breaths, their raised trunks searching the air, seeking scents muted by cold. They examined the sky. Kezia was first to sense my labour and she reached her trunk out to touch my body. The pains seized me and let go like a cross-stitch. She shuffled sideways to support me and when the pains came I bent forward, leaning my hands against her side as if it were a bed or a wall. Dust clung to her rough stiff hairs. I wanted to drop to the ground but she used her trunk to lift me, to urge me to stay on my feet. Kezia, from the land of endless heat, moved us all back through that dispassionate chill along the hard elephant path. They had to be put in the barn, shackled and settled in before my baby could be born.

There are, for most of us, a few singular moments around which we create the rest of our lives. People get stuck in them in all sorts of ways. Being born is a series of stucks. When Omega was born she moved quite nicely down the birth canal, push-stuck, push-stuck, push-stuck, until the very end when she didn't move any more. There we were, me and Omega, on the brink of a new life, stuck. Did she not want to be born? Did I not want my sleepy pregnancy to end? I remember pushing in a desultory sort of way and a strange woman's voice saying, "If you don't push her out I'm going for my knife!" I didn't really care what she said, I was too interested in my own pain, but an image of a blue baby began to fill the room.

In the centre of this cross-stitch of pain and rest, pain and rest, I glimpsed backwards into a time without self-reflection. I was body and mind undivided. The elephants have a sound for this: *waohm*. But I had to rouse myself out of my meditations and reluctantly push the baby out, sploosh! with a cry and a mighty heave.

When I held Omega a moment after the cord between us was cut I felt like a sacred hero at the end of a race. I also felt like a used-up tube of toothpaste. How could I feel these two things at the same time? But I did, caught between Omega's desire and my own. It has occurred to me that this is about ecstasy and garbage—a milky new baby in my arms, a lot of stinky blood on the floor. When she nursed we were skin to skin like throat singers humming and vibrating the sounds of each other against the world's darkness. Nursing and dripping in days and nights divided not by sun and moon but by seconds and minutes. I could hardly wait to show her to Kezia.

She had Jo's eyes.

With a child it is difficult to meditate. I have learned with Omega the fathomless worlds of meditating on Omega. *It's all for such a short time.*

I brought Omega to the barn when she was three days old. I unwrapped her, took off her diaper and let Kezia touch her all over. Her gentle trunk left a trace, her scent, on the baby. Kezia was chanting, *ooo ahahah~whoo aaohh.* I've never found a good translation of this sound. On that occasion it meant something like, *Be it unto me according to thy word.*

And so, I am still at the Safari. With a small baby it is easier to stop moving around so much. My migrations are interior wanderings as I cosy her on my back and take her walking with the elephants each day. I record the elephants chanting their nurturing songs over her and I've caught

Saba trying to lift her up from her blanket on the barn floor more than once. Her earliest inchoate memories will be of the scent of hay, the soft brush of an elephant's trunk. I have moved back into my mother's house and sleep there most nights. I made a nursery for Omega in my old room but she still sleeps with me. I'm going to build a summer aviary outside and soon I'll open up the studio. I am encouraging all of the elephants to draw and I'm going to sell their pictures instead of taking them to the circus. I suppose I have become one of those zoo people I used to find so eccentric. But when I take my Elephant-English dictionary to the university the zoologists and linguists find me odd too. I wonder, as time passes, if Jo would fit in if he ever came back. And I dream sometimes of Alecto. In the dreams he torments me, mouth agape, silently pulling me down until I awake in a sweat. Perhaps this is part of supplication, hope beyond memory.

I don't know how long I'll stay. When I get crumpled letters with bright yellow stamps from Zimbabwe I can smell the caves and feel the heat on my skin. But today, willing and fain, I ask the elephants to take me captive in their captivity, enthrall me and lead me hand in hand as we wander slowly through the hours watching a small baby grow, learning more and more of each other's language. There are nights when I chafe at my duties and fall battered into bed after working all day. There are days when I'm exhausted and I wish I had no one to take care of. But my ferocious love for this child and my deep bond with these elephants draw me into life, where old furies are gentled. The Safari will open again and the elephants have to be ready to walk among tourists, to make the trek down to the pond so that on summer afternoons people can marvel at the weightless joy they take in rolling and splashing in the water. I have to clean up the howdahs for the children's rides and get Saba's pictures framed. I have to take care of Omega. I want her to know where she will fall asleep and where she'll wake. Even in this small safari there is much to do. I find things to keep my heart occupied. Omega said her first word today. It was the greeting Saba makes to her, an audible *brah* with a light caress from her trunk. Omega waved her arms when Saba came up to us and made the sound back. Then they made the sound together and I listened and laughed to hear it. We are all each other's Word.

ACKNOWLEDGMENTS

When *Elephant Winter* was first published I was surprised at how many people asked whether the elephant lore in the novel is true. It is the job of fiction to give meaning to facts, and the job of language to shape the world. This being said, all of the elephant lore in the novel is drawn from extensive research into the history and mythology of elephants, accounts of their ability to communicate with each other and with humans, scientific studies on their physiology and behaviour, particularly their intense desire to learn and to nurture and teach their young.

I would like to thank Katy Payne for her extensive work on elephant communication and a generous afternoon she spent with me at Cornell University where she described her research and played me her audio and video tapes. Katy Payne was the first person to document elephant infrasound which she discovered by noticing a strange pressure change on her ear drums. She has continued her research on elephant communication in Africa as well as studies on their ability to teach each other migration routes. Her fine scientific work, and her admiration and knowledge of these great animals is an inspiration to me. It is important to stress however that while we understand elephants to have a small repetoire of infrasonic utterances with which they communicate, the Elephant–English Dictionary in this novel is a complete invention.

The work of many elephant researchers was important to me: Joyce H. Poole, Cynthia Moss, Iain and Oria Douglas-Hamilton, Heathcote Williams, Douglas Chadwick, H.H. Scullard, Ramesh Bedi. The autopsy notes are based on a 1936 report by Francis G. Benedict in *Physiology of the Elephant.* The ability of elephants to draw is described in David Gucwa and James Ehmann's *To Whom It May Concern: An Investigation of the Art of Elephants.* For the chance to see elephants in the wild I am grateful to the guides at Fothergill Island, Lake Kariba, in Zimbabwe. For access to elephants in captivity, I am grateful to Michael Hackenburger at the Bowmanville Zoo. For information on the training of elephants, and their habits in captivity, I consulted with several elephant keepers I met through the Elephant Managers Association. I have also turned to written accounts such as Franklin Edgerton's *The Elephant Lore of the Hindus.* One of my favourite descriptions of the qualities of an elephant driver comes from his book:

The supervisor of elephants should be intelligent, kinglike, righteous, devoted to his lord, pure, true to his undertaking, free from vice, controlling his senses, well behaved, vigorous, tried by practice, delighting in kind words, his science learned from a good teacher, clever, firm, ... fearless, all knowing.

Many ancient writers were interested in the physical and metaphysical significance of the elephant. I have read their observations avidly. Cassiodorus in *Variae* wrote, "Its breath is said to be a cure for headaches in man." Aelian in *De Natura Animalium* noted "An elephant will not pass by a dead elephant without casting a branch or some dust on the body." Livy, Oppian, Cassiodorus, Elder Pliny, Plutarch, Cicero all wrote about elephants. But my favourite of the ancients' observations belongs to Aristotle in *De Rerum Natura:* "The beast that passeth all others in wit and mind ... and by its intelligence, it makes as near an approach to man as matter can approach spirit."

Finally, I would like to thank the following for their generous encouragement and exchange of ideas: Rex Murphy, Leslie and Alan Nickell, Ann and Adam Winterton, Cynthia Holz and my writing group, Julie Showalter, and Carol Shields. Special thanks to Madeleine Echlin, Ross and Olivia Upshur and my publisher, Cynthia Good.